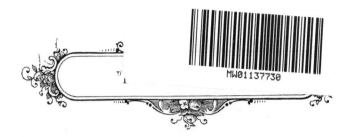

The Ladies Delight, Reduced into Rules of Practice

by

Michel Millot

[1655]

find more by typing

Locus_Elm_Press

at:

Amazon United Kingdom
Amazon United States of America
Amazon Germany
Amazon Netherlands
Amazon France
Amazon Spain
Amazon Canada
Amazon Australia
Amazon Brazil
Amazon Japan
Amazon Mexico
Amazon Italy
Amazon India

*

THE SCHOOL OF VENUS

The Ladies Delight, Reduced into Rules of Practice

by

Michel Millot

[1655]

Translated from the French, *L'Escole des Filles ou la Philosophie des dames*, anonymously in 1680

This paperback edition - Copyright: Locus Elm Press

Published: January 2017

TABLE OF CONTENTS

*

DEDICATION

To Madam S———W———

None Madam can be a candidate with you for this dedication, 'tis your Lordship alone has passed all the forms, and classes in this School, what delights you give, and with what eagerness you perform your Fucking exercises is sufficiently known to the many have enjoyed you, for you Madam like the Supreame Powers have such a communicative goodness, as you scorn monopolizing your Cunt to a single keeper, but have generously refused no Man a kindness who desired it, having often been heard to say 'twas not in your nature to deny satisfaction to a standing Prick, and that 'twas not barely thrusting a Prick into a Cunt, but the well managing of a Fuck makes the Summum Bonum. Tell not me therefore of Messalina, what though she was enjoyed by Fourty or Fifty Men in a day, if your Ladyship could command as many bodies as you have had Pintles between your legs, you might lead as great an Army as Xerxes did into Greece, or if a Pyramide of those standing Tarses your Cunt hath subdued were to be erected, I am confident it would exceed that Monument of Sculls erected, by the Persian Sophy in Spahaune, under your patronage therefore this Book comes abroad, and if it have your approbation I care not if other Ladies dislike it, Favourably therefore receive this Dedication from Madam

Your Most

Humble Servant

THE ARGUMENT

In the first Dialogue.

Roger a young Gentleman being passionately in love with Katherine a Virgin of admirable beauty, but so extremely simple, having always been brought up under the rigid Government of her Mother, who was Wife of a Substantial Citizen, that all his persuasions could do no good on her, by reason she understood not any thing that appertained to love, he therefore by force of presents and other allurements gains a Kins-Woman of hers named Frances to his Party, and she having promised Roger to solicit Katherine, in his behalf makes her a Visit.

Accordingly Frances who was much wiser than her Cousin, and better practiced in love concerns, undertakes Katherine whom finding opportunely at home, she cunningly acquaints the young Girl with all the pleasures of love, and by the relation so fired her blood as she longed to be at the sport, Frances then strikes while the Iron was hot, and persuades Katherine to embrace that opportunity, none being at home but herself and the Maid, and let Mr. Roger whose person she made agreeable to the young Wench, ease her of her Maidenhead, that the Girl consents to, and in the nick of time Mr. Roger coming to make a Visit, as Frances and he had before laid their design, FRANK.takes occasion to leave them alone.

In the Second Dialogue.

Katherine acquaints Frances, how she had lost her Maidenhead, the Variety of postures

Roger had put her in, and how afterward he had Swived her in various manners, besides all along in the discourse is inserted such Divine and Mysterious love Morals, as makes the Treatise very delightful and pleasant to the Readers.

THE ORTHODOX BULL

Anathema and Indulgence.

PRIAPUS, our most August Monarch, thunders forth Anathema against all manner of Persons of either Sex, who Read or hear Read the Precepts of Love, Explained in a Book called the School of VENUS, without spending or at least not having some incitements of Nature which tend to Fucking, on the other side he grants a Plenary Indulgence to all those who are debilitated by being superannuated, or having some other Corporal defect, he also gives his Benediction to all those Unfortunate Pilgrims who suffer for Venus's cause, and have therefore undertaken the Perilous Voyage of Sweating and Fluxing.

DIALOGUE THE FIRST

Frank. Katy.

FRANK. Good Morrow, KATY.

KATY. Oh! Good Morrow Cousin, and what good Wind blows you hither, now my Mother is from home. Lord how glad am I to see you. Is this Visit pure kindness or business?

FRANK. No business I assure you, but pure affection, I am come to chat and talk with you, 'tis wearisome being alone, and methinks, 'tis an age since last I saw you.

KATY. You say true, and I am much obliged to you, will you please sit down, you find no body at home but me and the Maid.

FRANK. Poor Soul, what thou art at work?

KATY. Yes.

FRANK. I think you do nothing else, you live here confined to your Chamber, as if it were a Nunnery; you never stir abroad, and seldom a man comes at thee.

KATY. You say very true Cousin, what should I trouble my self with men; I believe none of them ever think of me, and my Mother tells me, I am not yet old enough to Marry.

FRANK. Not old enough to be Married, and a young plump Wench of Sixteen; thou art finely fitted indeed with a Mother, who ought now to take care to please thee, as formerly she did herself, what's become of Parents love and affection nowadays, but this is not my business; art thou such a Fool to believe you can't enjoy a mans company without being Married?

KATY. Why, don't I enjoy their Company and do not men come often hither?

FRANK. Who are they? I never see any.

KATY. Lord! how strange you make it,

why is there not my two Unkles, my Cousins, Mr. Richards and many others?

FRANK. Pish, they are your kindred! I mean others.

KATY. Why, what make you of Mr. Clarke, Mr. Wilson, Mr. Reynolds, and young Mr. Roger, whom I ought to have named first, for he comes often and pretends he loves me, telling me a Hundred things which I understand not, and all to little purpose; for I have no more pleasure in their Company, then I have in my Mothers, or my Aunts. Indeed their cringes, congees and ceremonies, make me laugh sometimes, when I speak to them, they stare upon me, as though they would eat me; and at last go away like Fools as they came; what satisfaction can one receive by such persons Company? In truth instead of being pleased with them, I am quite a weary of them.

FRANK. But, do they not tell you, you are handsome, are they not perpetually kissing and stroaking thee?

KATY. Why, who the Duce told you? Indeed they do little else, but commend my beauty, kissing me and feeling my Breasts, telling me a Hundred things, which they say are very pleasing to them, but for my part, they add nothing to my content.

FRANK. Why, and do you suffer them to do all this?

KATY. Truly no, for my Mother hath forbidden me.

FRANK. Lord, what an ignorant innocent Fool art thou!

KATY. Pray Cousin, why do you say so, is there any thing to be learned, which I do not know?

FRANK. You are so ignorant, you are to learn every thing.

KATY. Sweet Cousin instruct me then.

FRANK. Yes, see, this is the fruits of being ruled by a Mother, and never mind what men say unto you.

KATY. What can an innocent Girl learn from men, whom the world account so debauched?

FRANK. I have a great deal of reason to speak well of them; for 'tis not long since I received a great deal of pleasure from one of that Sex; my dear Rogue, they are not half so bad as thou art made to believe, and the worst is, thou art never like to be convinced, thou art so cloistered up from their intrigues and Company, that thou wilt always live in ignorance, and consequently wilt never injoy any pleasure in this World: prithee tell me, what pleasure can'st thou injoy being always confined to a Chamber with thy Mother?

KATY. Do you ask me what pleasure, truly Cousin, I take a great deal, I eat when I am hungry, I drink when I am dry, I sleep, sing and dance, and sometimes go into the Country and take the Air with my Mother.

FRANK. This is something, but does not every body else do the like?

KATY. Why, is there any pleasure, that is not common to every body?

FRANK. Sure enough, for there is one that you have not yet tasted of, which as much exceeds all the rest, as Wine doth fair water.

KATY. Cousin, I confess my ignorance, in which I am likely to continue, unless you will please to explain it unto me.

FRANK. But, is it possible, that those men (especially Mr. Roger) with whom you have discoursed should not have said something of it unto you?

KATY. No indeed Cousin han't they, if this pleasure be so great, as you say, they have not had the charity to communicate it to me.

FRANK. What do you still doubt of the sweetness of it? It is the most sovereign pleasure we poor Mortals injoy; but I admire Mr. Roger, whom all the World thinks in love, which you did hear speak of it unto you; surely you do not answer his affection.

KATY. Truly Cousin, you are much mistaken, for he himself can't deny, but when he sighs and bemoans himself in my presence, I (far from being the cause thereof) pity him, ask him what he ailes, and should be glad with all my heart if I could give him any ease.

FRANK. Oh, now I begin to understand where the shooe wrings you both, why do not you tell him (when he professeth he loves you) that you also have a kindness for him?

KATY. Why so I would, if I thought it would do him any good, but since I know it is to no purpose, had not I better hold my peace?

FRANK. Alas Child, I can but pity thee, and thy misfortune, for if thou hadst but shewn some affection to him, he would without doubt have informed thee of this pleasure we are now talking of.

KATY. Prithee Cousin, how can that be, must a Maid of necessity love a man before she can attain to this pleasure? Methinks, I may love Mr. Roger and many men else, and yet not enjoy any pleasure in it.

FRANK. Yes, so you may you fool you, if people only look at one another, but there must be feeling in the case too.

KATY. Why, how many times have I touched him, and yet find no such pleasure in it?

FRANK. Yes, yes, you have touched his cloaths, but you should have handled something else.

KATY. Dear Cousin, expound your self

more clearly unto me, I understand not in the least what all this discourse tends to, tell me therefore in plain English, what must I do to attain this pleasure?

FRANK. Why then in short, 'tis this, a young Man and a Maid can without any cost or trouble give one another the greatest pleasure imaginable.

KATY. Oh, good Cousin, what a mind have I to know what this pleasure is, and how to enjoy it!

FRANK. Be not too hasty and you shall know all, did you never see a naked man?

KATY. I never saw a man in my life, I have seen little boyes stark naked.

FRANK. No, that will not do, the young Man must be Sixteen or Seventeen years old, and the Maid Fourteen or Fifteen.

KATY. If they must be so big truly then I never saw any.

FRANK. Dear Cousin, I love thee too well to keep thee longer in ignorance, did you never see a man at piss and the thing with which he pisseth?

KATY. Yes once I saw a man piss against

a Wall, who held something in his hand, but I could not imagine what it was, he seeing me look at him turned himself towards me, and then the thing he had in his hand, appeared to be like a white hogs pudding of a reasonable length, which was joyned to his Body, which made me admire I had not the like.

FRANK. And so much the better you Fool, for if you had, it was not possible for you to receive the pleasure we are now a talking of. But I am just now going to tell you things which will seem a great deal more strange unto you.

KATY. You oblige me infinitely, but pray first inform me, if this pleasure is singular, that none but a young Man and a Maid can partake thereof.

FRANK. No such matter, all People of all ranks and degrees participate therein, even from the King to the Cobler, from the Queen to the Scullion Wench, in short one half of the World Fucks the other.

KATY. This discourse is Hebrew to me, but is there no difference in this pleasure?

FRANK. Yes marry there is, Husbands and Wives take some pleasure, but they are generally cloyed with it, and therefore, sometimes the Wife, oftentimes the Husband ha's some variety by having a bit in a corner, as for example, your Father had often his pleasure of your Maid Servant Margaret, whom therefore your Mother when she perceived it, turned her away, and made such a clutter about t'other day, and yet, who knows but your Mother herself, who is yet indifferent handsome, may not have an Itching at her Tail, and have some private friend to rub it.

KATY. Of that matter I know nothing, but what mean you pray by Persons of Quality?

FRANK. Oh, there is the cream of the Jest, they are young Gentlemen that fly at all game, (London is full of them) neither Maid, Wife or Widow can escape them, provided they be tolerable handsome, and that their faces (according to the Proverb) will make sauce for their Arses. Neither want these young sparks employment, for the Town is never empty of these kind fucking Females;

generally both Sexes fuck, and that so promiscuously as Incest is accounted no sin, for they put it off with a Jest, saying it makes the top of their pricks look redder, if they dip it in their own Blood.

KATY. Because I am not Married, let us talk of young Men and Maids.

FRANK. Why, young Men and Maids take the most pleasure, because they are in their strength and youth, which is the season proper for these delights; but with which Sex shall I begin?

KATY. If you please let it be with the men.

FRANK. Be it so then, you must therefore know, the Thing with which a Man Pisseth is called a Prick.

KATY. Oh Lord Coz, you Swear?

FRANK. Pish, you are very nice, if you are minded to hear such Discourse, you must not be so Scrupulous.

KATY. I am contented, speak what you will.

FRANK. I must use the very words without Mincing, Cunt, Arse, Prick,

Bollocks, &c.

KATY. I am contented.

FRANK. Then let me tell you, the Thing with which a Man Pisseth, is sometimes call'd a Prick, sometimes a Tarse, sometimes a Mans Yard, and other innumerable Names. It hangs down from the bottom of their Bellys like a Cows Teat, but much longer, and is about the place where the Slit of our Cunt is through which we Piss.

KATY. Oh strange!

FRANK. Besides they have Two little Balls made up in a Skin something like a Purse, these we call Bollocks, they are not much unlike our Spanish Olives, and above them, which adds a great Grace to this Noble Member, Crows a sort of Downy Hair, as doth about our Cunts.

KATY. I very well apprehend what you say, but to what purpose have men all these things, sure they serve to some other use besides Pissing?

FRANK. Yes marry does it, for it is this very thing which giveth a Woman the delight I all this while have been talking of.

For when a Young Man hath a kindness for a Maid, he kneels down before her (when he hath gotten her alone) tells her he esteems her above all the World, and begs of her to answer his Love; if her silence continues, and she looks upon him with languishing Eyes, he usually takes courage, throws her backwards, flings up her Coats and Smock, lets fall his Breeches, opens her Legs, and thrusts his Tarse into her Cunt (which is the place through which she Pisseth) lustily therein, Rubbing it, which is the greatest pleasure imaginable.

KATY. Lord Cousin, what strange things do you tell me, but how the Duce doth he get in that thing which seems to be so limber and soft? Sure he must needs cram it in with his Fingers?

FRANK. Oh, thou are an ignorant Girl indeed, when a man hath a Fucking Job to do, his Prick is not then limber, but appears quite another thing, it is half as big and as long again as it was before, it is also as stiff as a stake, and when it's standing so stiff, the skin on the Head comes back, and it appears just like a very large Heart Cherry.

KATY. So when the Mans Prick stands, he thrusts it into the Wenches Hole.

FRANK. I marry does he, but it costs him some pains to thrust it in, if the Wench be straight, but that is nothing if he be a true mettel'd Blade, by little and little he will get it in though he sweat soundly for it, by doing of this Wench feels her Cunt stretch soundly, which must of necessity please her, seeing he Rubs and Tickles the Edges of it in that manner.

KATY. For my part I should think it would hurt one.

FRANK. You are mistaken, indeed at first it makes ones Cunt a little sore, but after one is a little used to it, it Tickleth and Rubbeth in such manner, as it yieldeth the greatest content and pleasure in the World.

KATY. What call you the Wenches Thing?

FRANK. In plain English it is called a Cunt, though they out of an affected modesty mince the word, call it a Twot, and Twenty such kind of Names. When a man thrusts his Prick into a Woman's Cunt, it is called Fucking. But pray don't talk of such kind of thing before Company, for they will call you an immodest bawdy Wench, and chide you for it.

KATY. Let me alone to keep my own Counsel. But still I am not satisfied, how a man can get his great Tarse into a Wenches Cunt.

FRANK. So soon as ever he hath put it a little into her Cunt Hole, he thrusts with his Arse backwards and forwards, and the Wench too is very charitable in helping him, so that between them both they soon get it up to the Head, and all the while the Man is Rigling his Arse, the Wench is extremely delighted.

KATY. I warrant, he never holds his Arse still.

FRANK. No, he still keeps on thrusting.

KATY. By this means I perceive he soon gets in.

FRANK. For example sake look upon me, and see how I move my Arse, just so do the men when they Fuck us, and all the time he is at it, the Woman plays with him, hugs him, and kisseth him, stroaks his Arse and Cods, calls him her Dear, her Love, her Soul, and all this while she is dying almost with pleasure, feeling his Prick thrust up so far into her Body.

KATY. Good Cousin, you speak so feeling of this pleasure, that I have a great mind to be trying the sport, sure if it be as you say, a Young Wench cannot but love the man that gives her so much delight, but have not the men their pleasure too?

FRANK. Yes, yes, that's easily perceived, they being almost mad with delight, for when they are at the sport they cry, Dear Rogue, I dye (sighing and breathing short) saying, where am I, and such amorous words, notwithstanding the Woman's pleasure is greater than the mans, because she is not only pleased with her own Fucking, but also hath the satisfaction of perceiving her Gallant so extremely delighted.

KATY. You speak a great deal of Reason, sure since they have so good sport, the

Wenches are loath to let the men get off of them, for my part were it my case, I should be very unwilling to let the Prick out of my Cunt, since it is the cause of such pleasure.

FRANK. Phoo, but that can't be.

KATY. Why so?

FRANK. When one Bout is done, you must Rest a little before you begin another.

KATY. I thought it had lasted as long as one pleased, and that there was no more in it than thrusting in the Prick.

FRANK. Therein you are mistaken, 'tis better as it is, for were it otherwise we should not be so happy.

KATY. Pray demonstrate all this Intrigue of Fucking unto me, how they end and begin again a fresh, and what is the natural Reason why the Prick being in the Cunt, should give such delight, and why should not ones Finger yield a Wench the like pleasure.

FRANK. Listen then. A Prick hath a fine soft loose skin, which though the Wench take it in her Hand, when it is loose and lank, will soon grow stiff and be filled: 'Tis full of Nerves and Gristles, the Head of the

Prick is compounded of fine Red flesh, much like a large Heart Cherry, as already I have told you, over this Head is a Cap of Skin which slips backwards when the Prick stands, underneath there is a pipe which swells like a great vain and comes to the Head of the Prick, where is a small slit or orifice; as for the Womans Cunt, I know not what it is within, but I am told it is nothing but a Prick turned inwards; now when a Prick thrust into a Cunt, the cap of skin which I before spoke of, and is called the prepuce slips backwards. This skin some Nations as the Jews and Turks cut off (calling it Circumcision) now as I told you, this Prick rubbing up and down in a Cunt, giveth the pleasure we have thus long discoursed of both to Man and Woman. In fine, what with rubbing and shuffing on both sides their members begin to Itch and Tickle; at last the seed comes through certain straight passages, which makes them shake their Arses faster, and the pleasure comes more and more upon them. At last the seed comes with that delight unto them, that it puts them in a Trance. The seed of the man is of a thick white clammy substance like suet, that of a Woman thinner and of a red color, mark, a woman may spend twice or thrice to a mans once, if he be any time long at it, some women have an art of holding the Tops of their Cunts, that they can let fly when they please, and will stay till the man spends, which is a Vast satisfaction to them both.

KATY. You describe this pleasure to be so excessive, that it puts me into admiration, but after all, what do they do when they have both spent?

FRANK. Then they are at ease for a little while, and the Prick which at first stood as stiff as a Stake, comes out of the Cunt pitifully hanging down its head.

KATY. I wonder at all this, but ha'nt they a mind to t'other touch?

FRANK. Yes, with playing, handling, and kissing, the Prick stands again, and then they stick it in again and have the same Sport.

KATY. But when the Prick is down, can a Wench make it stand again?

FRANK. Very easily, 'tis but gently rubbing it in her hand, if thou didst but know the virtue of a Wenches hand, and how capable 'tis of giving pleasure to a man, thou wouldest not wonder at it.

KATY. Pray Cousin, since you have taken the pains to instruct me thus far, leave me not in ignorance, and therefore inform me how this matter is completed!

FRANK. In short, 'tis thus, it often happens a couple of young lovers meet in some place, where they have not the convenience to fuck; they therefore only kiss and rub their tongues in one anothers mouths, this tickleth their lips and provokes the youth so, that it makes his Prick stand, they still continuing kissing, and it not being a convenient place to fuck in, he steals his Prick into her hand, which she by rubbing gently (which is called frigging) makes the man spend in her hand.

KATY. Hey day, what must a Woman of necessity know all these things?

FRANK. Yes, and a great deal more, for after a little repose they try another conclusion to please one another.

KATY. What another?

FRANK. Yes, another, she begins to stroke his coddes, sliding them between her fingers, then she handles his Buttocks and Thighs, and takes him by the Prick again, which certainly is no small delight unto him; after all what will you say if she gets upon him instead of his getting upon her, which I assure you pleases the man beyond any thing?

KATY. You tell me of variety of pleasures, how shall I do to remember them, how is it say you doth the Woman fuck the man?

FRANK. That is when he lays down backward, and Woman gets a stride upon him, and wriggles her Arse upon his Prick.

KATY. That's a new way, it seems this pleasure ha's many postures.

FRANK. Yes, above a Hundred, Have you but a little patience and I will tell you them all.

KATY. Why is the man more pleased when the Woman Fucks him, then when he fucks her?

FRANK. Because she is so charitable to take the pains and labor upon her, which otherwise had fallen to his share.

KATY. He is much beholding to her.

FRANK. Really so he is, for he lies under, receives the pleasure and takes no pains, whilst her eagerness at the sport makes her sweat till it drops again.

KATY. My fancy is so extremely raised by your very telling me how she bestirs herself, that I am almost mad to be at it.

FRANK. I have a great deal more to tell you, but let us make no more hast then good speed, for by a little and a little you will soon learn all.

KATY. I am very well satisfied, but methinks I would fain know what makes my Cunt Itch so (especially in the night) that I cannot take any rest for tumbling and tossing. Pray can you tell me what will prevent it?

FRANK. You must get you a stiff lusty Tarse to rub it, and must stick it into your Cunt, but if you have it not ready, you must rub your Cunt soundly with your finger, and that will give you some ease.

KATY. How say you with my finger? I cannot imagine how that can be.

FRANK. Yes with your finger, thrusting it into your Cunt, and rubbing it thus.

KATY. I'll be sure not to forget this way you tell me of; but did not you tell me you sometimes received a great deal of fucking pleasure?

FRANK. Yes marry did I, I have a fucking Friend in a corner, who swives me as often as I have a mind to it, and I love him extremely for it.

KATY. Truly he deserves it if he pleases you so much, but is your pleasure and satisfaction so great?

FRANK. I tell you, I am sometimes besides my self he pleaseth me so much.

KATY. But how shall I get such a fucking Friend?

FRANK. Why, you must be sure to get one that loves you, and one that will not blab, but keep your Council.

KATY. Do you know any body I could

trust in an affair of this nature?

FRANK. I cannot pitch upon any whom I think fitter for your turn than Mr. Roger, he loves you very well, and is a handsome young Fellow, had a good Jante mien is neither too fat or too lean, hath a good skin, strong and well set Limbs; besides, I am informed by those that know it, he hath a swinging Tarse and Stones, and has a strong back to furnish store of seed. In short, he is exactly cut out for a good Woman's Man.

KATY. I long to be dabbling, but still I am afraid there is some harm in it.

FRANK. Why, you will see I am not the worse for it.

KATY. Oh, but ain't it a sin and a shame to boot?

FRANK. You need not be half so scrupulous, I warrant you Mr. Roger can farewell and not cry roast meat, neither dares he betray you for fear of losing your kindness and his own Reputation.

KATY. But if it should be ones fortune to be Married after, I am afraid my Husband will not esteem or care for me, if he perceives any such matter.

FRANK. You need not take so much care beforehand, besides, when it comes to that, let me alone to tell you a way that he shall never perceive it.

KATY. But, if I should be found out my reputation is for ever lost.

FRANK. 'Tis a thing some with so much privacy, that it is impossible to be known, and yet every body almost doth it; Nay if the Parents themselves perceive it, they will say nothing but put off their cracked Daughter, to one Cocks-comb or another.

KATY. But they can't hide it from God, who sees and knows all things.

FRANK. God who sees and knows all things will say nothing, besides, I cannot think lechery a sin; I am sure if Women govern'd the world and the Church as men do, you would soon find they would account fucking so lawful, as it should not be accounted a Misdemeanor.

KATY. I wonder men should be so rigorous against a thing they love so well.

FRANK. Only for fear of giving too

much liberty to the Women, who else would challenge the same liberty with them, but it is fine, we wink at one anothers faults, and do not think swiving a heinous sin, and were it not for fear of great Bellys, it were possible swiving would be much more used then now it is.

KATY. Then you scarce think any honest?

FRANK. No really, for had not we better enjoy our pleasures, then be hard thought on for nothing, for I must confess there are some so unhappy as to be hard censured without a cause, which is the worst luck can befall one; were I in those Peoples condition, if I could not stop Peoples mouths, I would deserve the worst that could be said of me, and so have something for my Money.

KATY. You say very well, and truly I did not care how soon I parted with my Maiden-head, provided I might have my Belly full of fuck, and no body be the wiser, which I believe may easily be done, if according to your advice some discreet young Fellow be employed in management of this secret affair.

FRANK. You cannot imagine the satisfaction you will take, when once you have gotten a fucking Friend fitted for your purpose, who as I will order it shall be wise enough to keep your secrets. How many Girles do you daily meet with, who pass for virtuous Wenches, at these you may laugh in your sleeve, for they will never think thee to be a wanton, especially if thou dost but play the Hypocrite, acting the part of a Holy Sister, frequenting the Church and condemning the lewdness of the Age, this will get thee a Reputation among all sorts of People, and by thy private fucking thou wilt attain to a kind of confidence, which is much wanting to most of our English Ladies; for few are honest now a days but some heavy witless sluts, and after all, if thou behavest thy self as I will order, 'tis a thousand to one but some wealthy Fool will stoop to thy lute, and Marry thee, after which thou mayest carry on thy designs, and order private meetings with thy fucking Friend, who will secretly swive thee, and give thee all tastes of pleasure imaginable.

KATY. Lord Cousin, what a happy Woman are you, and what a great deal of time have I already lost, but pray tell me, how must I play my Cards, for without your assistance I shall never attain to what I so much desire?

FRANK. I'll endeavor to help you out of the mire, but you must FRANK.y tell me, which of your lovers you most esteem.

KATY. To be ingenious then, I love Mr. Roger best.

FRANK. Then resolve to think of no body else, for my part I think him a very discreet young Gentleman.

KATY. But, I am ashamed to break the Ice and ask the least kindness of him.

FRANK. Let me alone to do that, but when you have had the great pleasure of fucking, you must so order matters, that you may have frequent meetings, for when once you have tasted the forbidden fruit, your Teeth will be strangely set on edge after it.

KATY. I warrant you, you have so fired me with your Relations, that I think it seven years till I am at the sport.

FRANK. The sooner you do it, the better will Mr. Roger visit you to day.

KATY. Cousin, I expect him every minute.

FRANK. Without any more ado then, take this first opportunity, for a fairer can never present, your Mother and Father are in the Country and come not home to night, no creature in the house but the Maid, whom you may easily busy about some employment, and let me alone to do your errand to Mr. Roger, and to tell all People that may inquire for you, that you are gone abroad. Here's a bed fit for the purpose, on which he will certainly fuck you when he comes.

KATY. Dear Cousin, I am at my wits end, but must I let him do what he will with me?

FRANK. I marry must you, he will thrust his Prick into thy Cunt, and give thee a World of delight.

KATY. Well, but what must I do then to have as much pleasure as you have?

FRANK. You fool you, I tell you he'll

show you.

KATY. Excuse my ignorance, and Cousin to pass away the time till he comes, pray tell me what your Husband doth to you when he lies with you, for I would not willingly altogether appear a Novice, when I shall arrive to that great happiness of being fucked.

FRANK. That I will withal my heart, but you must know that the pleasure of fucking is joined with a Thousand other endearments, which infinitely add to the perfection, one night above all the rest my Husband being on the merry pin, shewed me a very many pritty pranks, which before I knew not, and which truly were pleasant enough.

KATY. When first he accosts you, what doth he say and do unto you?

FRANK. I will briefly tell you all, first, he comes up a private pair of stairs unto me, when all the Household is in Bed, he finds me sometimes a sleep and sometimes awake, to loose no time, he undresseth himself, comes and lies down by me, when he begins to be warm he lays his hands on my Breasts, finding me awake, he tells me he is so weary with walking from place to place all day long, that he is scarce able to stir, still feeling and streaking my Breasts, calling me dear Rogue, and telling me how happy he is in me; I thereupon pretending modesty say, dear heart, I am sleepy, pray let me alone, he not satisfied with that, slips his hand down to the bottom of my Belly, and handleth the heel of my Cunt, which he rubbeth with his fingers, then he kisseth me, and puts his Tongue into my Mouth delicately rolling it about, afterwards he strokes my smooth Thighs, Cunt, Belly and Breasts, takes the Nipples of my Breast in his Mouth, doing all he can to content himself, makes me take off my Smock and views me all over, then he makes me grasp his stiff Prick, takes me in his Arms and so we roll one over another, sometimes I am uppermost, sometimes he, then he puts his Prick into my hand again, sometimes he thrusts it between my Thighs, sometimes between my Buttocks, rubbing my Cunt with the top of it, which makes me mad for horsing, then he kisseth my Eyes, Mouth and Cunt, then calling me his Dear, his Love, his Soul, begets upon me, thrusting his stiff standing Tarse into my Cunt, and to our mutual satisfaction he fucks me stoutly.

KATY. And are not you mightily pleased at it?

FRANK. How can you imagine otherwise? You may see there are more ways then one to put a Prick into a Cunt, sometimes my Husband gets upon me, sometimes I get upon him, sometimes we do it sideways, sometimes kneeling, sometimes crossways, sometimes backwards, as if I were to take a Glister, sometimes Wheel-barrow, with one leg upon his shoulders, sometimes we do it on our feet, sometimes upon a stool, and when he is in Hast he throws me upon a Form, Chair or Floor, and fucks me lustily, so these ways afford several and variety of pleasures, his Prick entering my Cunt more or less, and in a different manner, according to the posture we Fuck in, in the day times he often makes me stoop down with my head almost between my Legs, throwing my Coats backwards over my Head, he considers me in that posture, and having secured the Door that we are not surprised, and makes a sign with his Finger that I stir not from that posture, then he runs at me with a standing Prick, and Fucks me briskly, and hath often protested to me he takes more pleasure this way than any other.

KATY. This last way of Fucking as are all others, (without doubt) must be extremely pleasant, and now I very well comprehend all you say unto me, and since there is no more in it than downright putting a Prick into a Cunt (though in divers postures) methinks, I could find out some new ways besides those you tell me of, for you know every Bodies Fancy varies, but let us now talk of that pleasant Night you had with your Husband in which he pleased you so extremely.

FRANK. Why that was but yesterday, in this Relation I shall tell you many Love Tricks which are common to us, who daily enjoy them, you must know I had not seen my Husband in Two days, which made me almost out of my Wits, when toward Twelve a Clock last Night I saw him steal into my Chamber, with a little Dark Lanthorn in his Hand. He brought under his Coat Sweetmeats, Wine, and such stuff to Relish our Mouths, and Raise our Lechery.

KATY. 'Tis needless to ask you whether the Apparition pleas'd you.

FRANK. He found me in my Petticoat, for I was not then a Bed, which hastily throwing up, he flung me backwards on the Bed, and with a stiff standing Tarse, Fucked me on the spot lustily, spending extreamly with Two or Three Thrusts.

KATY. Now I perceive we are most pleased when the Seed comes, and we take the most pains when we perceive it coming, and we never leave shaking our Arses till the precious Liquor comes.

FRANK. After the first Fuck I went to Bed, and he undressed himself, I was no sooner laid but I fell a sleep, (for you must know nothing provokes sleep so much as

Fucking) but he hugging me, and putting his Prick into my Hand, soon recovered me of my Drowsiness.

KATY. When a Mans Prick is once drawn, how long is it before it can stand again, and how often can a Man Fuck in one Night?

FRANK. You are always interrupting me! That's according to the Man you deal with, sometimes the same men are better at it than other times, some can Fuck and spend twice without Discunting, which pleaseth the Woman very much, some will Fuck Nine or Ten times in a Night, some Seven or Eight, but that is too much, Four or Five times in a Night is enough for any Reasonable Woman, those that do it Two or Three times spend more, and also receive and give more pleasure than those who do it oftener. In this case the Womans Beauty helps very much too, and makes the man Fuck a time or two extraordinary, but as in other pleasures, so in this, too much of it is for naught, and it commonly spoils young Lads and Parsons, Young Lads because they know not when they have enough, and Parsons because they think they never shall have enough, but that man that Fucks Night and Morning doth very fairly if he hold it, this is all I can say on this Subject. But you have interrupted me, and I know not where I left off.

KATY. You told me as you were going to sleep, he put his standing Prick into your Hand.

FRANK. Oh, I remember now, I feeling it stiff and buxom, had no more mind to sleep, but began to Act my part as well as he, and kept touch with him. I embraced him, and laying my heels on his Shoulders, we tumbled about and tossed all the Cloaths off, it being hot, we were so far from minding their falling, that we both stripped ourselves naked, we curveted a hundred times on the Bed, he still shewing me his lusty Tarse, which all this while he made me handle, and did with me what he would. At last he strows all the Room over with Rosebuds, and naked as I was, commanded me to gather them up, so that I turned my self in all sorts of postures, which he could easily perceive by the Candle which burned bright, that done, he rubbed himself and me all over with Jessimy Essence, and then we both went to Bed and played like Two Puppy-Dogs, afterwards, kneeling before him, he considered me all over with admiration, sometimes he commended my Belly, sometimes my Thighs and Breasts, then the Nobs of my Cunt, which he found plump and standing out, which he often stroked, then he considered my shoulders and Buttocks, then making me lean with my hands upon the Bed, he got astride upon me, and made me carry him; at last, he got off me, and thrust his Prick into my Cunt, sliding it down my Buttocks. I had no mind to let him Fuck me at first, but he made such moan to me, that I had no heart to deny him, he said he took a great deal of pleasure in rubbing the Inside of my Cunt, which he did, often thrusting his Prick up to the Head, then suddenly plucking it out again, the noise of which, it being like to that which Bakers make when they Kneed their Dow, pleased me extremely.

KATY. But is it possible such excessive Lewdness could please you?

FRANK. Why not when one Loves another, these things are very pleasant, and serve to pass away the time with a great deal of satisfaction.

KATY. Proceed then if you think it convenient.

FRANK. When he was weary of Tickling and Fucking me, we went as naked as we were born to the Fire side, where when we were set down, we began to drink a Bottle of Hypocras, and eat some Sweet-meats, all the while we were eating and Drinking, which did much Refresh us, he did nothing but make much of me, told me he dyed for love of me, and a hundred such sweet sayings, at last I took pity of him and opened my Thighs, then he shewed me his standing Prick, desiring me only to cover the Head of it with my Cunt, which I granting to him, we still eat on, sometimes putting what I was eating out of my mouth into his; at other times taking into my mouth what he was eating. Being weary of this posture we began another, and after that another, weary of this we Drank Seven or Eight brimmers of Hypocras, then being half Elevated, he shewed me all manner of Fucking ways, and convinced me there was as much skill in keeping Time a Fucking, as there was in Music; to be short, he shewed me all the Postures imaginable, and had we had a Room hung with Looking-Glasses to have beheld the several shapes we were in, it would have been the highest of contentment. Being now near satisfied, he shewed me and made me handle all his Members, then he felt mine. And last I desired him to make an end, took him by the Prick and led him to the Bed, and throwing my self Backwards, and pulling him upon me, having his Prick in my Hand, I guided, and he thrust it into my Cunt up to the Top, that he made the Bed crack again, I thrusting in due time every thing was in motion, his Prick being in as far as it would go, his Bollocks beat time against the Lips of my Cunt. To conclude, he told me he would give me one sound Thrust which should Tickle me to the Quick. I bid him do his worst, provided he made hast. All this while we called one another my Dear, my Heart, my Soul, my Life, Oh what will you do, pray make hast, Oh I dye, I can stay no longer, Get you gone, I can't endure it, pray make hast, pray have done quickly, you Kill me, what shall I do? And kissing me, he says, Oh, now, now, then giving me a home Thrust with his Tongue in my Mouth (I thinking my self to be in another World) I felt his Seed come Squirting up warm and comfortable into my Body. At which moment I so ordered my business, as I kept time with him, and we both spent together, it's impossible to tell you how great our pleasure was, and how mutual our satisfaction; but Cousin, had you been there, it would have made you laugh to see what variety of Faces were made in the Action.

KATY. I must need believe what you say, since the very Relation you have given me makes me mad for Horseing, in plain English my Cunt Itcheth like Wild-Fire, but what need all these preparations, I am for downright Fucking without any more ado.

FRANK. That's your Ignorance, you know not the delight there is in Husbanding this pleasure, which otherwise would be short and soon over. And now I think on it, since Mr. Roger will suddenly be here, I think it not amiss to instruct you a little more.

KATY. Yes, Pray Cousin, since we are gone so far, leave nothing Imperfect, and I shall be bound to Pray for you so long as I live.

FRANK. You must know then there are a thousand delights in Love, before we come to Fucking, which must be had in their due times and places; As for example, Kissing and Feeling are two very good pleasures, though much inferior to Fucking: Let us first speak of Kissing, there is the Kissing of our Breasts, of our Mouths, of our Eyes, of our Face, there is also the Biting or close Kiss, with Tongue in Mouth. These several Kisses afford different sorts of pleasures, and are very good to pass time away. The delight of Stroking and Feeling is as various, for every Member affords a new kind of pleasure, a fine white hard Round Breast fills the Hand, and makes a mans Prick stand with the very Thought of the Rest. From the Breasts we descend to the Thighs; is it not fine to stroke two smooth plump white Thighs, like two Pillars of Alabaster, then you slide your Hand from them to the Buttocks, which are full and hard, then come to a fine soft Belly, and thence to a Brave Hairy Cunt, with a plump pair of Red Lips, sticking out like a Hens Arse, now whilst the Man plays with the Womans Cunt, opening and shutting the Lips of it, with his fingers, it makes his Prick stand as stiff as a Stake: this member has also its several pleasures, sometimes it desires to be in the Womans hand, sometimes between her Thighs and Buttocks, and sometimes between her Breasts, certainly 'tis a great deal of satisfaction for Lovers to see those they are enamored of naked, especially if their members be proportional, and nothing provokes lechery more than lascivious naked postures. Words cannot express the delight Lovers take to see one another naked, what satisfaction then have they, when they come to fucking, it being the quintessence of all other pleasures. A moderate Cunt is better then one too wide or too little, but of the two a little straight Cunt is better than a flabby wide one. I'll have none of some of these last sort of Cunts, that if a man had an hell of a Prick they would scarce feel it. There is also a great deal of pleasure from the first Thrusting a Prick into a Cunt till the time of spending, and the sport be ended. First the mans rubbing his Prick up and down the Cunt hole, then the Woman kissing and embracing him with all the strength she hath, the mutual stroking, and lecherous expressions, struggling and cringings, the rolling Eyes, sighs and short breathings, Tongue kissing and making of love moan; 'tis admirable to see the activity of the body, and the faces they make when they are tickled. And now I have told you all that belongs to these pleasures, I think you are much beholding to me, for my part I am glad I have found you so docible a Scholar, and that you hear reason so well.

KATY. Truly Cousin, there is a great deal of it, and it is pretty hard to learn it all.

FRANK. Pish, I could tell you more, but I think I have told you enough for this time, but what think you of my Fucking Friend now?

KATY. Truly Cousin you are happy in him, and your merit deserves no less then the pleasure you receive by him.

FRANK. But I am sure you would praise him more, did you but know how secret, honest, and discreet he is, when we are in Company, he never looks upon me but with Respect, you would then by his deportment think he durst not presume to kiss my hand, yet when time and place give leave, he can change the scene, and then there is not a loose trick, but he knows and can practice to my great satisfaction.

KATY. Hush, hush, hold your peace.

FRANK. What's the matter? Do you aile any thing?

KATY. Cousin, my heart is at my Mouth, I hear Mr. Roger a coming.

FRANK. So much the better, cheer up,

what are you afraid of, I envy you your happiness, and the pleasure you will take. Come, be courageous, and prepare your self to receive him, whilst you settle yourself upon your Bed, as if you were at work; I warrant you, I'll prepare and give him his lesson, how he must carry himself to-wards you. In the mean time order your affairs so, that you be not surprised. God be with you.

KATY. Adieu dear Cousin, bid him use me kindly, and remember I am at your Mercy.

The end of the First Dialogue.

ADVERTISEMENT

The former Dialogue having given an account of many love mysteries, with the manner how to improve the delights and pleasures of Fucking. This second discourse shews the curious and pleasing ways, how a man gets a Virgins Maidenhead, it also describes what a perfect Beauty (both Masculine and Feminine) is, and gives instructions, how a Woman must behave her self in the ecstasy of swiving. 'Tis not unknown to all persons, who are devoted to Venus, that though our English Ladies are the most accomplished in the world, not only for their Angelical and Beautiful faces, but also for the exact composure, of their Shape and Body; yet being bred up in a cold Northern Flegmatick Country, and kept under the severe, though insignificant Government, of an Hypocritical Mother or Governess, when they once come to be enjoyed, their Embraces are so cold, and they such ignorants to the mysteries of swiving, as it quite dulls their lovers Appetites, and often makes them run after other women, which though less Beautiful, yet having the advantages of knowing more, and better management of their Arses, give more content and pleasure to their Gallants. This we see daily practiced, and indeed the only reason which makes many a man dote on a scurvy face is, because the woman is agreeable to his Temper, and understands these fucking practical Rules better, then a Young and Beautiful Wife. In short, I do appeal to any Gallant, who hath enjoyed an Italian or French woman, and commends them to the Skyes for their Accomplishments, if he would not leave the very best of them for an innocent Country

English Wench, if she were but as well skilled in the several fucking postures, as the former are. That my dear Country-Women (for whom I have a particular esteem) may not therefore be longer slighted, for their ignorance in the School of Venus as I translated the first Dialogue, so have I finished this to the ignorant Maid. I am sure this must be a welcome book, but if any Lady be in a superior class, then is in this School, I beg her pardon, and humbly entreat her in another Treatise, to well finish, what in this I have indifferently begun. And I am so confident of the Abilities of the English this way, that I am assured, if all of this nature, with what our voluptuous fucksters know, were communicated to the world, we need not translate French, or be at the trouble to read Aloisia, Juvenal, or Martial in Latine. But till some of them be kind, and do it favorably, accept of my endeavors.

DIALOGUE THE SECOND

Frank. Katy.

FRANK. I am glad to find you alone, and now pray tell me, how squares go with you, since last I saw you.

KATY. I thank you heartily, Cousin, I was never better in my life, and am bound to pray for you, spight of my precise Mother, who would fain make me believe Men are good for nothing, but to deceive innocent Virgins, I find the quite contrary, for my Gallant is so kind to me, that I want words to express it.

FRANK. I hope you do not repent then you have taken my counsel, I am sure Mr.

Roger will be damned before he be guilty of such a dirty action, as Babbling.

KATY. I am so far from repenting, that were it to do again, it should be my first work. What a comfort is it to love and be beloved? I am sure I am much mended in my health, since I had the use of Man.

FRANK. You are more Airy a great deal then before, and they that live to see it, will one day find you as cunning and deep a Whore, as any in the Nation.

KATY. Truly Cousin, I was a little shamefaced at first, but I grow every day bolder and bolder, my Fucking Friend assuring me, he will so instruct me, that I shall be fit for the embraces of a King.

FRANK. He is a Man of his word, and you need not doubt what he promises, what advantage have you now over other Wenches in receiving so much pleasure, which enlivens thee, and makes thee more acceptable in company.

KATY. I tell you what, since Mr. Roger has fucked me, and I know what is what, I find all my Mothers stories to be but Bugbears, and good for nothing but to fright Children, for my part I believe we were created for fucking, and when we begin to fuck, we begin to live, and all young Peoples' actions and words ought to tend thereunto. What strangely Hypocritical ignorants are they, who would hinder it, and how malicious are those old people, who would hinder it in us young people, because they cannot do it themselves. Heretofore what was I good for, but to hold down my head and sow, now nothing comes amiss to me, I can hold an argument on any subject, and that which makes me laugh is this, if my Mother chide, I answer her smartly; so that she says, I am very much mended, and she begins to have great hopes of me.

FRANK. And all this while, she is in darkness, as to your concerns.

KATY. Sure enough, and so she shall continue as I have ordered matters.

FRANK. Well, and how goes the world with you now?

KATY. Very well, only Mr. Roger come not so often to see me, as I could wish.

FRANK. Why, you are well acquainted with him then?

KATY. Sure enough, for we understand one another perfectly.

FRANK. But did not, what he did unto you at first, seem a little strange?

KATY. I'll tell you the truth, you remember you told me much of the pleasure and Tickling of Fucking, I am now able to add a great deal more of my own experience, and can discourse as well of it as any one. I am sure of my standing.

FRANK. Tell me then, I believe you have had brave sport, I am confident Mr. Roger cannot but be a good Fuckster.

KATY. The first time he Fucked me, I was upon the Bed in the same posture you left me, making as if I had been at work, when he came into the Chamber he saluted and asked me, what I did, I made him a civil answer, and desired him to sit down, which he soon did close by me, staring me full in the face, and all quivering and shaking, asked me if my Mother were at home, and told me he had met you at the bottom of the stairs, and that you had spoken to him about me, desiring to know if it were with my consent. I returning no answer, but Smiling, he grew bolder, and immediately Kissed me, which I permitted him without struggling, though it made me Blush as Red as Fire, for the Resolution I had taken to let him do what he would unto me, he took notice of it, and said, what do you Blush for Child, come Kiss me again, in doing of which, he was longer than usual, for that time he took advantage of thrusting his Tongue into my Mouth. 'Tis a folly to lye, that way of Kissing so pleased me, that if I had not before received your Instructions to do it, I should have granted him whatever he demanded.

FRANK. Very well.

KATY. I received his Tongue under mine, which he wriggled about, then he stroked my Neck, sliding his Hand under my Handkerchief, he handled my Breasts one after another, thrusting his Hand as low as he could.

FRANK. A very fair Beginning.

KATY. The End will be as good, seeing he could not reach low enough, he pulled out his Hand again, laying it upon my Knees, and whilst he was Kissing and Embracing me, by little and little he pulled up my Coats, till he felt my bare Thighs.

FRANK. We call this getting of Ground.

KATY. Look here, I believe few Wenches have handsomer Thighs than I, for they are White, Smooth and Plump.

FRANK. I know it, for I have often seen and handled them before now, when we lay together.

KATY. Feeling them he was overjoy'd, protesting he had never felt the like before, in doing this, his Hat which he had laid on his knees fell off, and I casting my Eyes downwards perceived something swelling in his Breeches, as if it had a mind to get out.

FRANK. Say you so Madam.

KATY. That immediately put me in mind of that stiff thing, which you say men Piss with, and which pleaseth us Women so much, I am sure when he first came into the Chamber 'twas not so big.

FRANK. No, his Prick did not stand then.

KATY. When I saw it, I began to think there was something to be done in good earnest, so I got up, and went and shut the Door lest the Maid should surprise us, who was below Stairs, I had much ado to get away for he would not let me stir till I told him 'twas only to make fast the Door; I went down and set the Maid to work in the Out-house, fearing she might come up and disturb us, if she heard any noise. Having made all sure I returned. and he taking me about the Neck and Kissing me, would not let me set as before upon the Bed, but pulled me between his Legs, and thrusting his Hand into the slit of my Coat behind, handled my Buttocks which he found plump, Round and hard, with his other hand which was free, he takes my right Hand, and looking me in the Face, put it into his Breeches.

FRANK. You are very tedious in telling your Story.

KATY. I tell you every particular. He put his Prick into my Hand, and desired me to hold it, I did as he bid me, which I perceived pleased him so well, that every touch made him almost expire, he guiding my Hand as he pleased, sometimes on his Prick, then on his Cods and Hair that grew about it, and then bid me grasp his Prick again.

FRANK. This Relation makes me mad for Fucking.

KATY. This done, says he, I would have you see what you have in your Hand, and so made me take it out of his Breeches, I wondered to see such a Damn'd great Tarse, for it is quite another thing when it stands, than when it lies down, he perceiving me a little amazed, said, do not be frighted, Girl, for you have about you a very convenient place to receive it, and upon a sudden pulls my Smock round about my Arse, feeling my Belly and Thighs, then he rubbed his Prick against my Thighs, Belly and Buttocks, and lastly against the Red Lips of my Cunt.

FRANK. This is what I expected all this while.

KATY. Then he took me by it, rubbing both the Lips of it together, and now and then plucked me gently by the hairs which grow about, then opening the Lips of my Cunt, he thrust me backwards, lifting my Arse a little higher, put down his Breeches, put by his Shirt, and draws me nearer to him.

FRANK. Now begins the Game.

KATY. I soon perceived he had a mind to stick it in; first with his Two Fingers he opened the Lips of my Cunt, and thrust at me Two or Three times pretty smartly, yet he could not get it far in, though he stroked my Cunt soundly. I desired him to hold a little, for it pained me, having Breathed, he made me open my Legs wider, and with another hard thrust his Prick went a little further in, this I told him pained me extremely, he told me he would not hurt me much more, and that when his Prick was in my Cunt, I should have nothing but pleasure for the pain I should endure, and that he endured a share of the pain for my sake, which made me patiently suffer Two or Three thrusts more, by which means he got in his Prick an Inch or two farther, endeavoring still to get more Ground, he so tortured me, as I cried out, this made him try another posture, he takes and throws me backwards on the Bed, but being too heavy, he took my Two Thighs and put them upon his Shoulders, he standing on his Feet by the Bed side. This way gave me some ease, yet was the pain so great to have my Cunt stretched so by his great Tarse, then once more I desired him to get off, which he did, for my part the pain was so great, that I thought my Guts were dropping out of the bottom of my Belly.

FRANK. What a deal of pleasure did you enjoy, for my part had I had such a Prick, I should not complain.

KATY. Stay a little, I do not complain for all this. Presently he came and kissed me, and handled my Cunt a fresh, thrust in his finger to see what progress he had made, being still troubled with a standing Prick, and not knowing what to do with himself, he walked up and down the Chamber, till I was fit for another bout.

FRANK. Poor Fellow, I pity him, he suffered a great deal of pain.

KATY. Mournfully pulling out his Prick

before me, he takes down a little Pot of Pomatum, which stood on the Mantle-tree of the Chimney, oh says he this is for our turn, and taking some of it he rubbed his Prick all over with it, to make it go in the more Glib.

FRANK. He had better have spit upon his hand and rubbed his Prick therewith.

KATY. At last he thought of that, and did nothing else, then he placed me on a Chair, and by the help of the Pomatum got in a little further, but seeing he could do no great good that way, he make me rise, and laid me with all four on the Bed, and having rubbed his Tarse once more with Pomatum, he charged me briskly in the rear.

FRANK. What a bustle is here to get one poor Maiden-head, my Friend and I made not half of this stir, we had soon done, and I near flinched for it.

KATY. I tell you the truth verbatim, my coats being over my Shoulders, holding out my Arse I gave him fair mark enough, this new posture so quickened his fancy, that he no longer regarded my crying, kept thrusting on with might and main, till at last he perfected the Breach, and took entire possession of all.

FRANK. Very well, I am glad you have escaped a Thousand little accidents which attend young lovers. But let us come to the sequel.

KATY. It now began not to be so painful, my Cunt fitted his Prick so well, that no Glove could come straighter on a mans hand; to conclude, he was overjoyed at his victory, calling me his Love, his Dear, and his Soul, all this while I found his Tarse Rub up and down in my Body, so that it tickled all the faculties of my Cunt.

FRANK. Very good.

KATY. He asked me if I were pleased, I answered, yes, so am I said he, hugging me close unto him, and thrusting his hands under my Buttocks, he lifted my Cunt towards him, sometimes handling the Lips thereof, sometimes my Breasts.

FRANK. This was to encourage or excite him.

KATY. The more he rubbed the more it tickled me, that at last, my hands on which I leaned failed me, and I fell flat on my face.

FRANK. I suppose you caught no harm by the fall.

KATY. None, but he and I dying with pleasure, fell in a Trance, he only having time to say, there have you lost your Maiden-head, my Fool.

FRANK. How was it with you? I hope you spent as well as he.

KATY. What a question you ask me, the Devil can't hold it when it is a coming, I was so ravished with the pleasure, that I was half besides my self, there is not that sweetmeat or rarity whatsoever, that is so pleasant to the Palate as spending is to a Cunt, it tickleth us all over, and leave us half dead.

FRANK. Truly, I believe you did not believe it half the pleasure you have found it.

KATY. Truly no, 'tis impossible till one has tried it. So soon as he withdrew, I found my self a little wet about my Cunt, which I wiped dry with my Smock; and then I perceived his Prick was not so stiffe as before, but held down it's head lower and lower.

FRANK. There is no question to be made of it.

KATY. This bout refreshed me infinitely, and I was very well satisfied, then he caressing and kissing me, told me what a deal of pleasure I had given him; I answered, he had pleased me in like manner, that he said more rejoiced him of any thing, we then strove to convince one another who had the most pleasure, at last, we concluded that we had each of us our shares, but he still said he was the better pleased of the two, because I was so well satisfied, which compliment I returned him.

FRANK. There is a great deal of truth in what you say, for when one loves another truly, they are better satisfied with the pleasure they give each other, then with that they themselves enjoy, which appears by a Woman, who if she really love a man, she will permit him to fuck her though she herself have no inclination thereunto, and of her own accord will take up her Smock, and say, get up dear Soul, and take thy fill of me, put me in what posture you please, and do what you will with me, and on the contrary, when the Woman hath a mind to be fucked, though the Man be not in humor, yet his complaisance will be as great towards her.

KATY. I am glad I know this, I will mind Mr. Roger of it as I see occasion.

FRANK. Therein you will do very well.

KATY. After a little pause, he got up his Breeches and sat down by me, told me he should be bound unto you so long as he lived, how he met you at the Stairs foot, where with your good news you rejoiced the very Soul of him, for without such tidings the Agony he was in for the love of me, would certainly have killed him, that the love which he had long time had for me, encouraged him to be doing, but he wanted boldness and Rhetoric to tell me his mind; that he wanted words to express my deserts, which he found since he enjoyed me to be beyond his imagination, and therefore he resolved to make a friendship with me, as lasting as his life, with a Hundred protestations of services he would do me, entreating me still to love him and be true unto him, promising the like on his part, and that he would have no friendship for any Woman else, and that he would every day come and Fuck me twice, for these compliments I made him a low Curtsey, and gave him thanks with all my heart. He then plucked out of his Pockets some Pistachios which he gave me to eat, telling me 'twas the best restorative in the World after Fucking; whilst he lay on the Bed, I went down to look after the Maid, and began to sing to take off all suspicion, I staid a while devising how to employ her again, I told her I was mightily plagued with Mr. Roger, and knew not how to be rid of him, yet found her out such work as assured me I should not be molested in our sport by her.

FRANK. In truth you are grown a forward Wench.

KATY. When I was got up Stairs again, I shut the door, and went to him, whom I found lying on the Bed, holding his standing Prick in his hand, so soon as I came, he embraced and kissed me, making me lay my powerful hand on his Prick, which did not yet perfectly stand, but in the twinkling of an eye it grew as stiff as a Stake, by virtue of my stroking.

FRANK. This we call rallying, or preparing to Fuck again.

KATY. I now began to be more familiar with it then before, and took a great deal of satisfaction with holding it in my hand, measuring the length and breadth of it, wondering at the virtue it had to please us so strangely; immediately he shuffles me backwards on the Bed, throwing up my coats above my Navel, I suffering him to do what he pleased, he seizing me by the Cunt, holding me by the hairs thereof, then turned me on my Belly to make a prospect of my Buttocks, turning me from side to side, slapping my Arse, playing with me, biting, tickling and reading love lectures to me all this while, to which I gave good attention, being very desirous to be instructed in these mysteries; at last, he unbuttoned his Breeches putting his Prick between my

Buttocks and Thighs, which he rubbed up and down, and all to shew me how to act my part when we Fucked in earnest.

FRANK. I am certain your Person and Beauty pleased him extremely.

KATY. That is not my discourse now. But he put me in a Hundred postures encunting at every one, shewing me how I must manage my self to get in the Prick farthest, in this I was an apt Scholar, and think I shall not in hast forget my lesson. At last we had both of us a mind to ease our selves; therefore he lay flat on the Bed with his Tarse upright, pulled me upon him, and I my self stuck it into my Cunt, wagging my Arse, and saying I Fuck thee, my dear, he bid me mind my business, and follow my Fucking, holding his Tongue all this while in my Mouth, and calling me my life, my Soul, my dear Fucking Rogue, and holding his hands on my Buttocks, at last, the sweet pleasure approaching made us ply one another with might and main, till at last it came to the incredible satisfaction of each party.

FRANK. This was the second bout.

KATY. Then I plainly perceived all that you told me of that precious liquor was true and knew there was nothing better than Fucking to pass away the time. I asked him who was the inventor of this sport, which he was not learned enough to resolve me, but told me the practice part was better than the Theory; so kissing me again, he once more thrust his Prick into my Cunt, and Fucked me Dog fashion, backward.

FRANK. Oh brave, this was the third time he Fucked you.

KATY. He told me that way pleased him best, because in that posture he got my Maiden-head, and besides his Prick this way went further into my Body then any other, after a little repose he swived me again Wheel-barrow fashion, with my Legs on his Shoulders.

FRANK. This was four times, a sufficient number for one day.

KATY. That was the parting Fuck at that time, in swiving me he told me, he demonstrated the greatest of his affection unto me.

FRANK. I should desire no better evidence, but how long did this pastime last?

KATY. 'Twas near Night before we parted.

FRANK. If you were at it less then three hours sure his Arse was on fire.

KATY. I know not exactly how long it was, this I am sure the time seemed not long to me, and if his Arse was on fire, I found an extinguisher which did his business. And this Cousin, is the plain truth of what hath befallen me since last I saw you, now tell me what is your opinion of it all.

FRANK. Truly you are arrived to such a perfection in the Art of Fucking, that you need no farther instructions.

KATY. What say you Cousin?

FRANK. Why I say you have all the Terms of Art as well as my self, and can now without Blushing call Prick, Stones, Bollocks, Cunt, Tarse, and the like names.

KATY. Why, I learned all this with more ease than you can Imagine, for when Mr. Roger and I am alone together, he makes me often name these words, which amongst

Lovers is very pleasing.

FRANK. Encunting is when one sheaths his Prick in a Cunt, and only thrust it in without Fucking.

KATY. But he tells me in Company modesty must be used, and these words forborne.

FRANK. In Truth, when my Friend and I meet, we use not half such Ceremonies as does Mr. Roger and you, tell me therefore, what is the difference between Occupying or Fucking, and Sheathing or Incunting?

KATY. Occupying, is to stick a Prick into a Cunt, and Wriggle your Arse till you Spend, and truly that word expresses it fuller than any other. Fucking, is when a Prick is thrust into a Cunt, and you spend without Riggling your Arse. Swiveing, is both putting a Prick into a Cunt, and stirring the Arse, but not Spending; to Encunt, or Ensheath is the same thing, and downright sticking ones Prick into a Cunt, beareth no other denomination, but Prick in Cunt.

FRANK. There are other words which sound better, and are often used before

Company, instead of Swiving and Fucking, which is too gross and downright Bawdy, fit only to be used among dissolute Persons; to avoid scandal, men modestly say, I kissed her, made much of her, received a favor from her, or the like; now let us proceed to the first Explication which you mentioned, and 'tis as good as ever I heard in my life. I could not have thought of the like my self.

KATY. You Compliment me Cousin, but I do not know well what you mean, they express Fucking by so many different words.

FRANK. That is not unknown unto me, for example, the word Occupying is proper when a man takes all the pains and labor, Encunting is called Ensheathing, from a similitude of thrusting a Knife into a Sheath. But men amongst themselves never use half these Ceremonies, but talk as Bawdy as we Women do in our Gossipings or private Meetings, if on one side we tell our Gossips or those that we trust in our amours, I Fucked with him and pleased him well, or he Fucked me and pleased me well, on the other side when they are among their Companions, they say of us, such a one has a Plagy wide Cunt, another tells of a straight Cunt, and the pleasure he received. 'Tis ordinary for two or three Young Fellows, when they get together, to give in their verdicts upon all the Wenches that pass by, saying among one another, I warrant you that jade will Fuck well, she looks as though she lacked it, she hath a Whoreish countenance, and also, if her Mouth be wide or narrow they make their descants thereon, looking on their Eye-brows, for 'tis very certain, they are of the same colour with the hair of their Cunts.

KATY. Oh, but will men reveal what they know of us?

FRANK. Yes, marry, of Common Whores they'll say any thing, but of their private Misses, the Gallants will be Damn'd before they will speak a word.

KATY. I am very glad of it, for I can scarce believe it of my self, that Mr. Roger should make me suffer so much Lewdness lately, and that I should suffer him to put me into so many Bawdy postures, truly I blush when I do but think of it.

FRANK. Yet for all your Blushes, you were well enough pleased with what he did unto you.

KATY. I cannot deny it.

FRANK. Well then, so long as you received no harm, there is no hurt done, if they did not love us, they would be Damn'd they would take the pains to put us into so many different postures.

KATY. You say true Cousin, and I am absolutely persuaded Mr. Roger Loves me very well.

FRANK. That you need not doubt of, since at first dash he tried so many several ways of Fucking thee.

KATY. I shall never forget a posture he put me the other day, which was very pleasant and Gamesome.

FRANK. I hope you will not conceal it.

KATY. No indeed, but when once you know it, I am confident you and your Gallant will practice it.

FRANK. Well, what is it?

KATY. Last Sunday in the Afternoon, my Mother being gone to Church, he having not seen me in Three days before, gave me a visit. So soon as he came in, being impatient of delay, he flung me on a Trunk and Fucked me; having a little cooled his courage, we Kissed and dallied so long, that his Prick which he showed me stood again as stiff as a Stake, then he flung me backwards on the Bed, flung up my Coats, opened my Legs, and put a Cushion under my Arse, then Leveling me right, he took out of his Pocket Three little pieces of Red, White, and Blue Cloths, the Red he put under my Right Buttock, the White under my Left, and the Blue under my Rump, then looking me in the Face, he thrust his Prick into my Cunt, and bid me observe Orders.

FRANK. This was a good beginning.

KATY. Yes, but it had a better Ending.

FRANK. Let me know how.

KATY. As he thrust, if he would have me lift up my Right Buttock, he called Red, if the Left Buttock, he called White, if he meant my Rump, he called for Blue.

FRANK. Oh brave, what perfection art thou arrived at.

KATY. Till he was well settled in the Saddle, he was not over Brisk, but soon as he was well seated, he cried out like a Mad man, Red, Blue, White, White, Blue, Red, so that I moved Three several ways to his One, if I committed any mistake, he gentled reproved me, and told me that then I mistook White for Blue, or Blue for White. I told him that the Reason was, because the Blue pleased me more than any of the other.

FRANK. The Reason was, because that the Blew being in the Middle, that motion made him thrust his Prick farthest.

KATY. I perceive you know too much Cousin, than to be instructed by me.

FRANK. However go on, perchance I may learn something.

KATY. What would you have more? At last he holding his Tongue in my Mouth let fly, but he was so long at his Sport, that I spent twice to his once; at last he taught me a Trick to hold my Seed till he was ready to spend, when he was, we spoke both with frequent Sighs and short breaths, so that when the Liquor of Life came, we scarce knew where we were.

FRANK. Indeed they that at Spending make the least noise give the more pleasure, though some cannot abstain from it, and to excuse it say, that it is pleasure.

KATY. What do they mean, is it pleasure to make a noise, or doth the pleasure they receive by Fucking cause it?

FRANK. My opinion is, that Fucking maketh them do it, for why may not great pleasure have the same effect upon us, as great pain hath, and you know Tickling often makes us cry.

KATY. How comes this to pass?

FRANK. They get upon Wenches sitting bolt up right with their Pricks in their Cunts, with a grim countenance, like St. George on Horse back, and so soon as they find the sperm come Tickling, they cry out, oh, there, there, heave up, my Love, my Dear, thrust your Tongue in my Mouth. To see them in that condition would make one who knoweth not the Reason, come with Spirits to help fetch them to life again, believing they were ready to dye.

KATY. Sure the Wench is very well satisfied, to see the man make so many Faces, provided the parties can fare well and not cry Roast Meat, that is, be very secret, I think the pleasure very lawful.

FRANK. We were saying that the height of pleasure makes men cry out, I tell you so do Women too very often, for when they find it coming, they often Roar to the purpose, crying out, my Dear Rogue, thrust it up to the Head, what shall I do, for I dye with pleasure. Such Blades and Lasses Fuck in some private place, where they cannot be heard. Now some are such Drowsy Jades as nothing will move.

KATY. Say you so, pray what sort of Animals be they?

FRANK. Why such as must be prompted by Frigging, and other ways to Raise their Lechery, but when once their Venery is up, their Cunt is like the Bridge of a Fiddle, which makes them mad for Horsing.

KATY. But do not they Spend?

FRANK. Yes, they can't hold it, but Spend more than others.

KATY. That Wench, whose Gallant is so dull as he must want her Assistance to make his Prick stand, is very unhappy

FRANK. Now let us speak of them that do not spend with Fucking. First Eunuchs, whose Stones are cut out, their Pricks stand now and then, but they cannot emit any Seed, and yet their Pricks will so tickle, as they can make a Woman Spend, and Women in Turkey formerly made use of them, till of late a Turkish Emperor seeing a Gelding cover a Mare, Eunuchs now have all Pricks and Stones cut off.

KATY. I abominate all these sort of People, pray don't let us so much as mention them, but let us talk of those Lads, who have swinging Tarses to please Women.

FRANK. By and by, but I have not yet mentioned some People who say nothing in their Fuckings, but Sigh and Groan, for my part I am for those that are mute, those that make a noise being like Cats a Catterwauling.

KATY. But what part doth Woman act whilst she is Fucking with the man?

FRANK. Don't run too fast, and thou shalt know all at last. Let us consider what progress we have made, we are now no forwarder than the manner of thrusting a Prick into a Cunt, and the pleasure there is in Spending, with the satisfaction of Kissing, handling, and other Love Tricks, of which we have not fully spoken, nor of its due time and place when to be practiced. This therefore shall be your this days Lesson, it being a very material thing, and of great consequence, for 'tis the chief end of Love, and the way how to please men.

KATY. Without doubt Cousin all this must be most excellent, and 'tis even that wherein I desire to be informed.

FRANK. Let us put the case then. Thou wer't at handy Gripes with thy Lover, and didst not know how to make good the skirmish, whilst he is a laboring on thee, you must speak low with little affected Phrases, calling him your Heart, your Soul, your Life, telling him he pleaseth you extremely, still minding what you are about, for every stroke of your Arse affords a new pleasure, for we do not Fuck brutally like Beasts, who are only prompted thereto for Generations sake by nature, but with knowledge and for Loves sake. If you have then any Request to make to the man, do it when he is at the height of his Lechery, for then he can deny the Woman nothing, and nothing mollifies the Heart more than those Fucking Actions; Some Jades have been so fortunate as to Marry Persons of Great Quality, merely for the knack they had in Fucking; These Love Toys extremely heighten a mans Venery, who therefore will try all ways to please you, calling you his Soul, his Goddess, his little Angel, nay he will wish himself all Tarse for thy sake, so soon as he finds it coming, he will not fail to give thee notice of it by his half words and short Breathings; Remember these things I have told you, and look to your bits.

KATY. I warrant you, let me alone, but what posture do you usually put your self in?

FRANK. For the most part you must thrust your Buttocks towards him, taking him about the Neck and Kissing him, endeavoring to Dart your Tongue into his Mouth, and Rowling under his, at last clinge close unto him, with your Armes and Legs, holding your Hands on his Buttocks, and Gently Frigging his Cods, putting his Arse to you to get in his Prick as far as you can, thou knowest what follows as well as I can tell thee, only mind to prepare thee as I have informed you, and he will make mighty much of you, and though he give himself and all he is worth unto you, yet will he not think he hath done enough for you.

KATY. Cousin, though your obligations are great, yet I poor Wench have nothing but thanks to return you, but the postures you have informed me of, I shall make use of as opportunities present, that my Gallant may perceive I love him.

FRANK. 'Tis a common fault among young People only to think of the present Time, but they never consider how to make their pleasures durable, and to continue it a long time.

KATY. Let me have your instructions, who are so great a Mistress in the art of Love.

FRANK. But ha'nt you had Mr. Rogers company lately?

KATY. Now and then I used to let him in, and he lay with me a whole night, which happiness I have been deprived of above this Fortnight, for my Mothers Bed being removed out of her Chamber, (which is Repairing) into mine, so that our designs tending that way have been frustrated ever since.

FRANK. But you see him daily, do you not?

KATY. Yes he visits me daily, and Fucks me once or twice if there be time, now one time was very favorable unto us, for the Maid being gone abroad, my Mother bid me open the Door for him, which I did, and because we would not loose that opportunity, but take fortune by the forelock he thrust me against the Wall, took up my Coats, made me open my Thighs, and presented his stiffe standing Tarse to my Cunt, shoving it in as far as he could, plying his Business with might and main, which pleased me very well, and though I was very desirous of the sport, yet he made a shift to spend before me, I therefore held him close to me, and prayed him to stay in me till I had done too, when we both had done, we went up Stairs, not in the least mistrusting any thing. But when my Mother was from home, we took our Bellies full of Fuck, if my Mother or any Company was in the House we watched all opportunities that he might encunt me, we were both of us so full of Fuck, that we did not let slip the least minute that was favorable unto us; nay more; we sometimes did it in fear and had the ill luck to be disturbed and forced to give over our sport without spending, if it proved a false alarm we went at it again, and made an end of our Swiving; sometimes we had the ill fortune, that in two or three days time he could only kiss and feel me, and we thought it happiness enough if we could but make Prick and Cunt meet, which if we did they seldom parted with dry Lips. At other times if we sat near one another, he would pull out his Prick throwing his Cloak over it, and with languishing eyes shewing it me standing, in truth I could but pity him, and therefore drew near him, and having tucked up my Smock, he thrust his hand into my Placket and felt me at his will, tickling my Cunt soundly with his finger, when he was once at it, he held like a Mastiffe Dog and never left till he made me spend. This is called Digiting and if rightly managed give a Woman the next content to Fucking, this way he did to me, but the better is thus ordered. After a Wench is soundly swived, and that her Arse is wet with seed, the Man must keep her lying on her Back, then taking up the Lip of her Cunt, thrust in his finger into the hole through which she pisseth, (which is above the Cunt hole, and is made like the Mouth of a Frog) and then the Woman must be soundly frigged, which will make her start, and give her so much pleasure that some esteem it beyond Fucking. We grew every day more learnedly then the other, so that at last we found out a way of Fucking before Company, without being perceived by any of them.

FRANK. Pray tell me how that is?

KATY. As I was once Ironing, my Mother being gone out of the Room, he came behind me, pulls up my Cloaths and puts his Prick between my Thighs, striving to get it into my Cunt; I feeling him labouring at my Arse, ne're minded what I was doing, so that I burnt a good Handkerchief by the means, when he saw he could not this way get his Prick in, he bid me bow down and take no farther care, for he would give me warning if any body came, but I going to stoop, he found the slit of my Coat behind, so small that it displaced his Prick, which made him curse and swear, because he was forced that time to spend between my Thighs.

FRANK. What pity was that.

KATY. When the job was over and he had put up his tool again, I began to murmur at the ill fortune I had in burning my Handkerchief, which my Mother hearing, comes up and calls me Idle Huswife, protesting she would never bestow any more upon me, but Mr. Roger made my peace again, for he told my Mother, that it was done whilst I ran to the Window to see what was doing in the streets, not dreaming the Iron had been so hot.

FRANK. But all this while, you have forget to tell me the new way you have found out to Fuck before Company.

KATY. The manner we found it out was thus, Mr. Roger gave me a Visit one Night, as we were dancing with some few of our Neighbors, he being a little frustrated with Wine set himself on a Chair, and whilst others danced, feigned himself a sleep; at last he pulled me to him, and sat me down on his knees, discoursing with him about ordinary matters, keeping my eyes fixed on the Company all the time, all this while having thrust his Hand in at my Placket behind, he handled my Cunt, whilst I felt his stiff standing Tarse thrusting against me, which he would fain have thrust through the slit of my Coat behind, but that was not long enough for him to reach my Cunt, and he dare not pull up my Coats, the Room was so full of Company. At last with a little Penknife he pulled out of his Trousers, he made a hole in the exact place, and thrust his Prick into my Cunt, which I was very glad of; we went leisurely to work, for we dare not be too busy for fear of being caught, though I received a great deal of pleasure, yet I held my Countenance pretty well, till we were ready to spend, when truly I was fain to bite my Lip, it tickled me so plaguily. An hour after, he Fucked my Arse again in the same manner, this way we often since before Company experimented, and I have often thanked him for his new invention.

FRANK. Ah but this way is hazardous, and for all your biting of your Lip the Company might take notice of you, 'twere better therefore for you to hold down your head, and keep your hand before your Face, for then they could not perceive any thing, and would only have thought your head had Ached.

KATY. You say very true Cousin, and I shall observe that way for the future, indeed

I must confess I have learned more of you then any one else, in this mystery of Fucking, and shall always acknowledge it.

FRANK. Nay since you are my Scholar 'tis my duty to make you perfect, if therefore you want any more instructions pray be free with me and ask what you will.

KATY. After all these pleasures we have talked of, I perceive 'tis that part of a man which we call Prick contents us Women best; now I would fain learn of you, what sorts of Pricks are best and aptest to satisfy us.

FRANK. You propound a very good and pertinent question, and I will now resolve it unto you. You must know then though there are Pricks of all sorts and sizes, yet are they briefly reduced to these three sorts, great ones, midling ones, and little ones.

KATY. Let us begin with the little ones, how are they made?

FRANK. They are from four to six Inches long, and proportionally big; these are good for little, for they do not fill a Cunt as it should be, and if a Woman should have a great Belly, or have a flabby Cunt with a great pair of Lips to it, (which is a great perfection) or if the Cunt hole be low, which is a fault on the other side, it is impossible for such a Prick for enter above two or three inches, which truly can give a Woman but little satisfaction.

KATY. Well but what say you to the great ones?

FRANK. Great horse Tarses hurt and open a Cunt too wide, nay they often pain tried Women as well as Virgins, such is their strange bigness and length, that some men are obliged to wear a Napkin or cloth about them, to hinder then from going in too far.

KATY. Well what say you to the midling Pricks?

FRANK. They are from Six to Nine Inches, they fit Women to a hair, and tickle them sweetly. As in Men so in Women too, there are great, small, and middling Cunts, but when all is done be they little or great, there is nothing so precious as a friends Prick that we love well, and though it be no longer then ones little finger, we find more satisfaction in it then in a longer of another mans. A well sized Prick must be reasonable big, but bigger at the Belly then at the Top, there is a sort of Prick I have not yet mentioned, called the Belly Prick, which is generally esteemed above the rest; It appears like a snail out of it's shell, and stands ofter then those large Tarses which are like unwieldy ladders, which take a great more time to Rear then little ones.

KATY. I have another question to ask you.

FRANK. What is it pray?

KATY. Why do Men when they fuck us, call us such beastly names? Methinks they should court and complement us, I cannot conceive how love should make them so extravagant.

FRANK.'Tis love only that makes them use those expressions, for the greatest and chiefest cause of love, is the pleasure our Bodies receive, without that there would be no such thing as love.

KATY. Pray excuse me, there I know you will tell me of Brutal love, and that may be, but there is other besides which you may know by it's lasting, whereas Brutality endures no longer then any other extravagant Passion, and is over so soon as the seed is squirted out of the Prick.

FRANK. Why then all love is Brutal, which I will plainly demonstrate unto you.

KATY. Pray take the pains to do it, and I will not interrupt you.

FRANK. Though the pleasure passes away, yet it returneth again, and it is that which cherisheth love, let us come to the point, would you love Mr. Roger if he were gilt, and would you esteem him and think him a handsome Man, and fit for your turn, if he were impotent? What say you?

KATY. Truly no.

FRANK. Therefore don't I speak truth, and if you had not a Cunt too for him to thrust his Prick into, and Beauty to make it stand, do not deceive yourself and think he would love you for any other good quality. Men love to please themselves, and though they deny it, believe them not, and the chief mark they aim at is our Cunts; also when we embrace and kiss them, we long for their Pricks, though we are ashamed to ask it, for notwithstanding all the Protestations of honor, the tears they shed, the faces and cringes they make, it all ends in throwing us backwards on a Bed, insolently pulling up our Coats, and catching us by the Cunts, getting between our legs and Fucking us. In short, this is the end of all; most commonly those that love most, swive least, and they that Fuck oftest have seldom a constant Mistress, if they have, the love doth not last long, especially if the Mistriss were easily gained. 'Tis strange to see Women pretend to love with constancy, making it such a virtue, protesting that it is not Fucking they delight in, when we daily see them use it. To be short, all ingenious persons confess, that copulation is the only means of generation, and consequently the chief procurement of love.

KATY. How learned are you Cousin in these mysteries of love, pray how came you by all this knowledge?

FRANK. My Fucking friend takes a great

deal of delight to instruct me, and love hath this excellency in it, that though at first we do not think of Swiving, yet is it the chief thing we aim at, and the only remedy to cure love.

KATY. You have said as much on this Subject, as possibly can be expected.

FRANK. Now the reason why Men call us Women such beastly names, when they Fuck us, is because they delight in naming such things as relate unto that pleasure, for when they are in the Act of Fucking, they think of nothing but our Cunts which makes them express themselves accordingly, saying my Dear Cunny, my little Fucking fool, my pretty little Tarse taker, and such like words which they use in the Act of Venery. This also proceeds from the attentiveness of our Spirits, when we are in copulation, and gives a lively Representation of the mind on the beloved object; for our very Souls rejoyce at these amorous embraces, which appears by the sweet union of two Tongues, which tickle one another in soft murmurs, pronouncing my Dear Dove, my Heart, my very good Child, my Chicken; all these are Emblems of affection, as my Dove, when they consider the Love of Pigeons, good Child and Chicken, relate to the dearness of a Child, and harmlessness of a Chicken my Heart, that is, they so passionately love the Woman that they wish they could reach her Heart with their Prick. In fine, all the words they use are like so many Hieroglyphics, signifying every one of them a distinct sentence, as when they say my Cunny, it signifies they receive a great pleasure by that part, and you might add innumerable similitude more. There are also very sufficient reasons, why they call every thing by it's right name, when they are Fucking us.

KATY. How say you Cousin?

FRANK. First the more to celebrate their Victory over us, as when they once enjoy us they take pleasure to make us blush with those nasty words. Secondly their thoughts and imaginations being so intent on the pleasure they take, they can scarce speak plain, and as they breath short, they are glad to use all the Monosyllabic words they can think of, and metaphorise as briefly as they can upon the obscene parts what they usually called Loves Paradise and the center of delight, they now in plain English call a Cunt, which word Cunt is very short and fit for the time it is named in, and though it make Women sometimes Blush to hear it named, methinks indeed they do ill, that make such a pother, to describe a Monosyllable by new words and longer ways then is necessary, as to call a Man's Instrument according to it's name, a Prick, is it not better than Tarsander, a Mans-yard, Man Thomas, and such like tedious demonstrations, neither proper nor concise enough in such short sports. For the heat of love will neither give us leave or time to run divisions, so that all we can pronounce is, come my dear Soul, take me by the Prick, and put it into thy Cunt, which sure is much better then to say, take me by the Gristle, which grows at the bottom of my Belly, and put it into thy loves Paradice.

KATY. Your very bare narration is able to

make ones Cunt stand a tip toe, but after all this, would you persuade me that Mr. Roger, only loves me for Fucking sake?

FRANK. I don't say it positively, there is reason in all things, sometimes the Woman's wit and breeding is as delightful as her Body. They help one another, some love for their Parts, some for mere Beauty. I have heard my friend say sometimes, when he hath heard me maintain an argument smartly, he was mad to be Fucking me on the spot, the cleverness of my wit so tickled him, that he could not rule his stiff standing Tarse, but desired to thrust it into my Body to reach the soul of me, whose ingenuity pleased him so much.

KATY. I now find my self pretty well instructed in love tricks, and in all the intrigues Men use tending thereunto, but now let us speak of Maids, who are equally concerned with men in love, what is the Reason that they are so coy and scrupulous to be kissed, nay though we make them believe 'tis no sin to kiss?

FRANK. Oh, but they are fearful of being

got with Child.

KATY. What if I should be with Child? The abundance of sperm Mr. Roger hath spurted into my Cunt makes me mistrust it.

FRANK. Pho fear no colors, if ever that happens I'll help thee out, for I have infallible remedies by me, which will prevent that in time of need.

KATY. Pray Cousin let me have them.

FRANK. And so you shall if there be occasion, but to ease you of that fear and trouble, first know that these misfortunes are not very frequent, that we need not fear them before they happen. How many pregnant Wenches are there, that daily walk up and down, and by the help of Basques and loose garbs hide their great Bellies till within a Month or two of their times, when by the help of a faithful Friend they slip into the Country, and rid themselves of their Burthen, and shortly after return into the City as pure Virgins as ever? Make the worst of it, 'tis but a little trouble, and who would loose so much fine sport for a little hazard, sometimes we may Fuck two or three years and that never happen, and if we would be so base 'tis easy to have Medicines to make us miscarry, but 'tis pity such things should be practiced in this time of Dearth, and want his Majesty hath of able Subjects, in which there are none more likely to do him Service then those which are illegitimate, which are begot in the heat of Lechery.

KATY. I shan't so much for the future fear a great Belly, this I am sure of, it cannot but be a great satisfaction to a Woman, that she hath brought a Rational and living creature into the World, and that one whom she dearly loves had his share in getting it.

FRANK. You say very true, against the time of your lying in, 'tis but preparing a close and discreet Midwife, and after the Child is born have it nursed by some Peasants Wife in the Country till the Child be grown up and provided for, either by Father or Mother.

KATY. But, what do those poor creatures do, who are so fearful to be got with Child, that though their Cunt tickleth never so much, yet dare they not get a lusty Tarse to rub it, for methinks fingering is unnatural.

FRANK. Why may be they have another way to please themselves.

KATY. What way pray can that possibly be?

FRANK. I have somewhere read of a Kings Daughter who for want of a Prick in specie, made use of a pleasant device, she had a brazen statue of a Man painted flesh color, and hung with a swinging Tarse composed of a soft substance, hollow, yet stiff enough to do the business. It had a red head and a little hole at the Top, supplied with a thwacking pair of Stones, all so neatly done, it appeared natural, now when her desire prompted her, she went and eased nature, thrusting that Masquerade Prick into her Cunt, taking hold on the Buttocks, when she found it coming, she pulled out a spring, and so squirted out of the Prick into her Cunt a luke warm liquor, which pleased her almost as well as Swiving.

KATY. Lord, what can't leachery invent?

FRANK. And no doubt but Men in their Closets have statues of handsome women after the same manner, which they make use of in the same way and rub their standing Pricks in a slit, at the bottom of their bellies proportionally deep, and in imitation of a Cunt.

KATY. This is as likely as what you said before, but pray go on.

FRANK. Wenches that are not rich enough to buy statues must content themselves with dildos made of Velvet, or blown in glass, Prick fashion, which they fill with luke warm milk, and tickle themselves therewith, as with a true Prick, squirting the milk up their bodies when they ready to spend, some mechanic jades frig themselves with candles of about four in the pound; Others as most Nuns do make use of their fingers. To be short, Fucking is so natural, that one way or another Lechery will have it's vent in all sorts and conditions of People.

KATY. This is pleasant enough, go on with your story.

FRANK. Some Women that fear Child-bearing will not Fuck, and yet they will permit their Gallants not only to kiss them, but also to feel their skin, Thighs, Breasts, Buttocks and Cunts frigging the Men with their hands, rubbing their Cunts and bottom of their Bellies with the sperm, yet they will not permit the Man downright swiving.

KATY. What is next?

FRANK. There are a sort of bolder Jades, who will suffer themselves to be Fucked till they feel the sperm coming, when immediately they will fling their rider out of the Saddle, and not suffer him to spend in them; some will tie a Pigs Bladder to the Top of their Pricks, which receives all without hazard. Some are so confident of their cunning, that they will let Men spend in them, but they will be sure it shall be before or after they have done it themselves, for all Physicians agree they must both spend together to get a Child, yet after all, most Women put it to hazard, and rather venture a great Belly than receive the pleasures but by halves, and stop in their full career, who certainly are in the Right, for of a hundred Women that Fuck, scarce Two of them prove with Child, for my part, those that will follow my advice, should neither trouble themselves with care either before or after Fucking, for such fears must certainly diminish the pleasure, which we ought rather to add unto, for there is not the like content in this World as entirely to abandon ones self to a party Beloved, and to take such freedom and liberty one with another, as our Lust shall prompt us unto.

KATY. Though I believe Cousin you are weary with Discoursing, yet I must needs ask you another question or two before we part.

FRANK. You hold me in a twined Thread. Ask what you please.

KATY. By the Symptoms you tell me of I am afraid I am with Child, for when ever Mr. Roger Fucks me we spend together, to give our selves the greater pleasure, now can you tell me any sign, or do you know any Reason why I should not be with Child?

FRANK. Yes marry can I, for besides spending together, the Woman if she have a mind to take, must shrink up her Buttocks close together, and lye very still till the Man have done, did you do so?

KATY. For matter of holding my Buttocks together, that I always do, but 'tis impossible for any so Airy a Wench as I am, to hold my Arse still in the midst of so great pleasure, no, I always shake it as fast as I can for the Heart of me.

FRANK. That alone is enough to prevent it, for stirring so much disperseth the Mans Seed, and hindereth it from taking place, that it cannot possibly joy in with the Woman's, as for holding our Buttocks close, that none of us can help, for it is consistent with the pleasures we receive, to keep them as close as we can. Now Nature which maketh nothing in vain offereth us a better mark at the Cunt, thrusting it towards the Man, so that the Lips of the Cunt entirely Bury the Mans Tarse that makes your Experienced Fucksters cry, Close, Close, which is to say, close behind and open before.

KATY. I improve more and more by your Discourse, as to my being with Child you have satisfied me, being not at all afraid of it, but pray tell me why men had rather we should handle their Pricks more than any other part of their Bodies, and why they take so much pleasure to have us stroke their Cods, when they are Fucking of us?

FRANK. That's easily answered, for 'tis the greatest Satisfaction they receive, nor can we better make them sensible of the satisfaction they give us. Is it not reason to make much of a thing which gives us so much pleasure? 'Tis also very obliging and grateful to the man; A Woman's hand hath great virtue in it, and is an Emblem of Love for Friends when they first meet shake hands, now the Love of Man and Woman is more natural, for thence the body and mind partake; in short, though a Woman suffer a Man to Fuck her, spend in her, and have his will of her in every thing yet if she don't take him by the Prick, 'tis a sign she cares not so much for him nay, she ought when her Gallant is Fucking of her, and thrust up his Tarse as far as he can into her, to feel the Root of his Prick and make much of his

Bollocks, and Nature hath ordered it so, that a Man at once receiveth Two pleasures one from the Cunt, the other from the Hand, there being a great part of the Prick behind the Stones which never entereth into the Cunt, but reacheth to a Mans Arsehole. This was so placed purposely for the Woman to handle it when she is in the very act of Venery. There is nothing belonging to the Privy parts, but if we consider good reason may be given why it is so, and to what use it serves, Nature having made all things in it's perfection to please us, if we know the true use of them. I have enlarged a little more on this Subject, because it hath some Relation to my concerns, I and my Fucking Friend having often experimented those feeling pleasures. Is it not Child a fine sight to see a little piece of limber Flesh, which hangs down at the bottom of our Friends Belly to grow stiffer and stiffer, till it be as hard as a Stone, and all this by virtue of Hand stroking?

KATY. This Question being now resolved, pray tell me, who hath the most pleasure in Fucking, the man or the Woman?

FRANK. That's hard to resolve, but if we look upon the running out of the Seed to be the material cause, then certainly the Woman hath most, for she feels not only her own, but the Mans too, but the Man feels only what comes from himself but this Question cannot easily be resolved, because the man cannot be Judge of the Womans pleasure, nor she of the Mans.

KATY. But how comes it to pass, that both Sexes Naturally love and desire Copulation, before they have any experience or tryal of its pleasure?

FRANK. Man and Woman were ever joined together from the beginning, and Copulation was ordered for the propagation and continuance of Mankind, to which Nature hath added so much delight, because the thing in it self is certainly so nasty, that were it not for the pleasure, certainly none would commit so filthy an act.

KATY. What is it you call Love?

FRANK. 'Tis a desire one half hath to unite it to the other half.

KATY. Pray take the pains to make this more plain unto me.

FRANK. 'Tis a Corporal desire or the first motion of nature, which by degrees ascends up to Reason, where it is perfected into a Spiritual Idea; so that this Reason finds an absolute necessity of uniting one half to the other half, when nature hath what she Requires, that Idea or spiritual vapor by little and little dissolves it self into a white liquid substance, like Milk which tickling softly down through our Backbones into other Vessels, at last becomes the pleasure of which before 'twas the only Idea.

KATY. What causeth that Idea to tickle so in it's passage?

FRANK. Because it pleaseth her, that she is nere communicating her self to the beloved object.

KATY. Truly this is admirable, but why can't People (in the height of lechery) laugh since they are both so well pleased?

FRANK. Because the head partakes not of their pleasures, for all the Joy is divided between Cunt and Prick.

KATY. This makes me smile.

FRANK. But you may think otherwise of it?

KATY. How mean you?

FRANK. The Soul by the violence of this great pleasure descends and thinks no more of it self, but leaves the functions of reason empty and unprovided, now laughter being a propriety of reason is with it anticipated, which is thus proved, when the Idea begins to pass through our Vessels, we find a kind of drowsiness and stupefaction of our senses, which demonstrates the privation of the soul from those parts, and the pleasure being so great in our secret members, it is not in the souls power to exercise any other faculty.

KATY. Though these Lectures are very Learned for a young Schollar, yet will I reflect on them, but why do Men thrust their Pricks between our Breasts, Thighs and Buttocks, when we won't suffer them to put them into our Cunts, certainly this is a kind of blind love, for which I cannot imagine a true reason?

FRANK. You have given it an excellent Epithet (you remember what I said before of the Idea) for the Members of the Woman is the part of the Man, Love being blind and not knowing where the conjunction is, provided, that the Man partake in it's pleasure in the conjunction of each Member, so that the Man finding the pleasure coming, frigs and rubs himself against the Woman, cheating his Reason by the Idea to which that conjunction hath some resemblance, with what is true and natural to it, he is transported if in the beloved object, he feels any thing that makes the least resistance to his Prick, which makes him shuffle on harder and harder.

KATY. You have cleared this point Cousin, but we have not yet spoke of Tongue kissing, which I reckon nothing but a mere fancy

FRANK. Tongue kissing is another cheat, which desireth conjunction in any manner whatsoever, 'tis a true resemblance and representation of the Prick entering into the Cunt, the Tongue slides under another

Tongue, but in so doing finds a little resistance by the lips of the recipient, and the resemblance of this object cheats the mind the better to imitate the Pricks entrance into the Cunt. When these kind of caresses are made, 'tis then we breath out our very hearts and Souls out of our Mouths for it makes the lover think that his Prick should go after the same manner into the Cunt of her whom he kisseth, and I believe the Womans thoughts are not much unlike the Mans; in short, they do what they can to imitate Swiving after the liveliest manner, they can with their Tongues, which they thrust and roll about in one anothers Mouths, as if they were a Fucking.

KATY. Enough, enough of this Cousin, or else you'll make me spend but why is the pleasure greater when the Woman gets upon the Man and Fucks him, then when she is passive and lyes under?

FRANK. I have already given you one Reason, and now I will give you another; 'tis a Correspondence of love, for Man and Woman you know are perfect and distinct

Creatures, now the great love they bear one to another makes them desire to transform themselves one into the other.

KATY. But still you do not tell me why they Fuck Topsie Turvy, and the Woman is a top who ought to be under.

FRANK. Yes but I have, but if there were no other reason this is sufficient, she ought not perpetually to work him at the labor Oar.

KATY. I grant all this.

FRANK. Besides, it is a kind of Metamorphosis, for when the Woman is a top, the Man is possessed with feminine thoughts, and the Woman with Masculine passions, each having assumed the contrary Sex by the postures they are in.

KATY. This is according to a former lesson you taught me, which I think I shall not forget.

FRANK. Pray, what was that?

KATY. That one half desireth to be united to the other half.

FRANK. 'Tis an assurance of a good principle, when the reasons and effects of the causes we infer are well deduced.

KATY. I think we have spoken enough of all things relating to love, and therefore I think we may rest here.

FRANK. I agree with you in that particular, but pray be careful then not to forget any of your lessons.

KATY. To help my memory pray then make me a short Repetition.

FRANK. First, we have spoken of the Effects which are stroking, handling and kissing, then of the thing it self, and several ways of Conjunction, the several humors of Men and Women, their dispositions and sundry desires, we have unfolded love with its nature, properties and effects, it's uses how and in what manner it acts it's part, and the reasons of it, and I am sure if we have omitted any thing it cannot be of much consequence. Indeed there may be a Hundred other little particular love practices, which now we have not time to enumerate, first as to the uniting of one half to the other, the desires and ways of doing it, the tickling, Arse-shakings, cringes, sighings, sobbs, groans, faintings away, hand clappings, and sundry other caresses, of some of which we have already spoken; so that we will now make an end, and if there be any thing remaining, discourse it at another meeting.

KATY. Well Cousin, give me your hand upon it.

FRANK. Why, I promise you I will. What needs all this pother between you and I?

KATY. Well, I can but give you thanks, for the great favors you have done me, in thus instructing me.

FRANK. What needs all these compliments, do you know what you have thanked me for?

KATY. For the patience you have had all this while to instruct my thick soul in all these love lessons, and of those most excellent reasons you give for every thing, making me perceive what an inexhaustible Fountain love is, this I am sure of, I never could have had a better informer to instruct me from it's first Rudiments, to it's highest notions imaginable.

FRANK. Pray no more of your compliments, love hath this excellency in it, that it entirely satisfies every body, according to their apprehensions, the most ignorant receiving pleasure though they know not what to call it; hence it comes, that the more expert and refined wits have a double share of it's delights, in the soft and sweet imaginations of the mind. What pleasant thoughts and sweet imaginations occur, when we are at the sport, and now it comes in my mind, I like this way of the Woman's riding the Man beyond any other Posture, because she takes all the pains the Man ought to do, and maketh a Thousand grimaces, as the pleasure doth tickle her, and the Man is extremely happy, for he seeth every part of the beloved upon him, as her Belly, Cunt and Thighs, he seeth and feeleth the natural motion she hath upon him, and the steadfast looking in her Face adds fuel to his fire, so that every motion of her Arse, puts him in a new ecstasy, he is Drunk with pleasure, and when love comes to pay the tribute which is due to their pleasures, they are both so ravished with Joy, they almost expire with delight. This is a Subject one might amply enlarge on if there were time.

KATY. 'Tis impossible to represent every bodies imagination upon this subject, for methinks I could invent more postures then you have told me of, and as pleasing unto me, but pray whilst you are putting on your Scarfe to be gone tell me one more thing.

FRANK. Well, what is it?

KATY. What is it will make two lovers perfectly enjoy one another?

FRANK. Truly, that will require more of me then the putting on of my Scarfe, first we must talk of Beauty, which they must both have, then we must come to other particulars, which are too long to treat of now.

KATY. However grant me my request, for the longer you are with me the greater is my pleasure, it is not so late, but you may stay a little longer, the truth is, you have put me so agog this day, that I can endure to talk of nothing but what relates to love.

FRANK. Well, I will do this, provided when I have done you will keep me no longer, you have almost sucked my well dry, turn up the glass, for upon my word I will stay no longer then this half hour.

KATY. Then I will make the better use of my time, Cousin, I know not how it comes to pass, but when I am absent from my friend I always think of the pleasant pastime I have in his company, and not considering his other perfections, I am so strangely besotted with his Stones and Prick, that ever and anon I am fancying he is thrusting it into my Cunt, with all the force he hath, stretching my Cunt as a Shoemaker doth a straight Boot, sometimes, I think it tumbleth the very coggles of my heart, these imaginations make me so damnable Prick proud, that I spend with the very conceit of them.

FRANK. This Ordinarily happens to all Lovers, and is a product of your desire, which Represents things of this Nature, so lively unto you, as if they were Really such, and your thinking of your Friends Prick more than any other part, plainly sheweth, that whatever Idea we have of the Person whom we Love, which Love brings into our minds, thoughts of the Privy Members, as being the cause of the immediate pleasure we take, the other Members though never so Beautiful, being but circumstances: As for example, a fair Black Eye, a fine White plump Hand, and a delicate Taper Thigh, makes a man consider the Cunts admirable structure, strangely exciting sensual Appetites, and make the Prick stand, which cannot any other ways be eased but by spending.

KATY. I understand this very well, but Cousin, since Beauty was the Subject we were upon, pray describe it unto me, and Represent a perfect enjoyment accompanied with all the pleasures that go along with it.

FRANK. Beauty consists in Two things, first in the perfect and well proportioned lineaments of the Body, and secondly of the Actions thereunto belonging.

KATY. I am much taken with these clear Divisions.

FRANK. There are some Women, which though they cannot properly be called handsome, yet have they such a Jointy mien as the French term it, as renders them extremely taking.

KATY. To talk of each feature is too tedious, my desire is only to have Beauty described.

FRANK. Then will I begin with the Woman, and then speak of the Man. She must be a Young Lass of Seventeen or Eighteen years Old, pretty plump, and a little inclined to fat, straight, and of a good Statue and Majestic looks, having a well proportioned and noble Face, her Head well set on her Shoulders, sparkling Eyes, with a sweet and pleas ant Aspect, her mouth rather of the bigger size than too little, her Teeth even and very White, her forehead indifferent, and without frowns, her Cheeks well filled up, Black Hair and a Round Face, her Shoulders Large and of a good breadth, a fine plump and smooth Neck, hard Breasts, that hang not down, but support themselves like Ivory Apples, an Arm proportional to the rest, a skin neither too White nor too Tawny, but between both, and so filled with flesh that it hang not loose, a

Hand White as Snow, and well set on at the Wrists; as to her Manners, first let her be neatly Drest, Modest, yet with lively Actions, let her words be Good and Witty, she must appear Innocent and a little ignorant before Company, and let her manage all her Discourse so, that it may tend to ingratiate her self with the hearers, and make her Person the more taking, still to keep her self within the bounds of modesty, and not to give the least encouragement to any to violate it, and if by chance any should offer an uncivil action or discourse to her, she must protest she knows not what they would be at, or what they mean, at Public Meetings and Feasts let her be very demure, let her Eat and Drink but moderately, for you may know the humor of the Lass, as she is more or less affected with pleasures, and inclined to Diversions, which her words and Actions will easily detect, therefore excess is dangerous to Young Women, but if it be the General Frolick of the Company, she may indulge her self a little more liberty, especially if she be amongst those who have a good Repute in the World; to make her more complete, she must Dance well, Sing well, and often Read Love Stories and Romances, under pretense to learn to speak well her Mother Tongue, she ought to have a tender Heart, even when she Reads of cruelty, though in one of these Romances.

KATY. You have made an admirable Description of a fine Woman.

FRANK. I have not yet done with all the Perfections of the Body, but come to describe her naked, she must have a fine hard Belly well thrust out, for 'tis upon this delightful Rock where all Lovers are Shipwrecked, her Stomach must be soft and Fleshy, fine small feet turning out at the Toes, which shews that her Cunt is well situated, her Calf of her Leg Plump and large about the middle, small and short Knees, substantial and Tapered Thighs, on which must hang a pair of Round hard Buttocks, a short Rump, and a slender Waste, the Reins of her Back very pliable for her Cunt sake, the heel of her Cunt must be full and hard, round beset and Trimed with dark coloured hair, the slit of her Cunt ought to be Six Fingers below her Navel, the skin whereof must be well stuffed out and slippery, so that when a Mans Hand is upon it, he cannot be able to hold it still in one place, but it will slide and come down to the two Lips of her Cunt, which ought to be red and strut out, the Cunt hole ought to be of an exact bore to do Execution, and so contrived, that the Prick having forced the first Breast work, may come to the Neck of the Cunt, and so farther forcing before it the small skins, and getting half in, then having taken breath, they both strive again till the Noble Gentleman has got Field Room enough, and at last arrives at the entrance of the Matrix, where my fair Deflowered Virgin will find abundance of Tickling pleasure, but I speak of so perfect a Beauty, that her Gallant will be besotted with her, till he comes to have a fling at her Plumb Tree.

KATY. Having thus described a Lass in her full and Blooming Beauty, what must be the perfections of the Man, which when you have informed me according to your

Doctrine, we will put the Two halves together?

FRANK. To be short, he must be of a fair Stature and a strong able body, not of a Barbary shape like a Shotten Herring, which is proper to Women only, let him have a Majestic Gate, and walk decently, a quick pleasing Eye, his Nose a little Rising, without any deformity in his Face, his Age about Five and twenty, let him rather incline to Lean than Fat, his Hair of a dark Brown and long enough to Curl upon his Shoulders, a strong Back and double Chested, let him be indifferently strong, so that he may take his Mistress in his Armes and throw her upon a Bed, taking up her Two Legs and flinging them over his Shoulders, nay he ought to Dance and handle her like a Baby, for it often happens, a Young Spark may have to deal with a Refractory Girl, who will pretend so much modesty, as she will not open her Legs, so that if he have not strength to force her, he will Spend in the Porch, and not Rub her Cunt with his stiff standing Tarse, he must have a well fashioned Foot, and a well proportioned Leg with full Calves, and not like Catsticks, and a pair of lusty Brawny Thighs to bear him up, and make him perform well. What, you seem to wonder at this? Oh, did you but know how enticing strong and vigorous Masculine Beauties are, especially when united to a Neat and perfect Feminine one, you would wish to enjoy no other pleasure, what a brave sight it is to see the Workman of Nature sprout out at the bottom of a Mans Belly, standing stiffly, and shewing his fine Scarlet Head, with a Thwacking pair of Stones to attend it's motion, expecting every minute the word of Command to fall on. I warrant it would alarm thy Cunt, which I would have thee always keep in readiness, that it may be able and ready to withstand the briskest onset the stoutest Tarse of them all can make: Be not afraid of having thy Quarters beaten up, though the Prick be never so big, indeed it may scare a tender Young Virgin, for it Thunders such a ones Cunt hole, and carries all before it.

KATY. What pretty sweet cruelty is this.

FRANK. I tell you 'tis a Perfection in a man to have a Tarse so big that it will scare a Virgin, and this in short is the Description of a Complete Man.

KATY. Now demonstrate unto me a perfect enjoyment of persons qualified according to your Description.

FRANK. In the Act of Copulation, let them both mind all manner of conveniences, the Wench must in some things appear a little shame-faced, the Man cannot be too bold, yet I would not have her so bashful as to deny him when he demands Reason, and what belongs to Love: I would only have her modestly infer by her Eyes, that she hath a mind to do that which she is ashamed to Name, let her keep at a little distance, to egge on her Gallant, and make him the more eager, 'tis not becoming the Wench to prostitute her self, though she is glad to hear her Gallant often beg that of her, which she within her self wisheth he would desire; therefore the Man must have a quick Eye and regard all her Actions, Sighs and words, that so nothing she wants may escape his knowledge, but so soon as ever he hath Encunted, 'tis then past time to consider, but let him mind his Knitting, and wag his Arse as fast as he can, whilst she will shame-facedly hold down her Head and wonder at the Sweet Ravishment he commits on her Body. Let him make full and home thrusts at her Cunt, and let her lay ready to receive them, with her Legs as far a sunder as possible, if she is not much used to the sport, probably her Cunt at first may smart a little, or else impossible she may complain out of pretended modesty, but let him not fear, for the hurt she receiveth will not be so great as the pleasure. If his Prick be never so big, if it do but stand stiff enough to make way 'twill enter at last, and the pleasure will be the greater; therefore the Wench ought to be very Tractable, and not refuse to put her self in any posture he shall demand of her; she should also encourage, Kiss him, and speak kindly unto him, cheering him up till he have finished the work he hath in Hand. I would have the Wench let the Man have a full Authority over her, and let her Body be totally at his disposal, let what will happen. She will at length find a great deal of sweet in it, for he will instruct her in what is fitting, and force her to nothing incongruous to Love and it's pleasures, if she be a seasoned Whore, she is to blame if she play the Hypocrite, and pretend modesty after her so long continuance in Fornication, and thereby loose a great deal of pastime. To conclude, I would have no Woman Tantalize a Man with her Hand, since she hath a more proper place to receive and bestow his Instrument, and 'tis a thousand pities so much good stuff should be lost, if she does indeed think the Mans Prick too big, she must for Love of him take the longer time, and try often anointing his Prick with Pomatum, and make use of all the other means she can imagine, and no doubt, in the Conclusion, be it never so big, she will get it in to both their contents.

KATY. These lectures Cousin, which you read unto me are far different from those my Mother Preaches, they treat of nothing but virtue and honesty.

FRANK. Yes, yes, Cousin, so goes the World now adays; lies overcome truth, reason and experience, and some foolish empty sayings are better approved of then real pleasures. Virginity is a fine word in the Mouth, but a foolish one in the Arse, neither is there any thing amiss in Fornication but the name, and there is nothing sweeter then to commit it; neither do Married People refrain, but run at Mutton as well as others, and commit Adultery as often as others do Fornication: Prick and Cunt are the chief actors in the Mystery of Love, the Ceremony is still the same, but I have said enough for once, and must not now pretend to reform the World, some are wiser than some, and the fools serve like foiles to set off the wise, with more advantage. But always take notice, the greatest pleasure of Swiving is secrecy, for thereby we keep a good reputation, and yet enjoy our full swinge of pleasure.

KATY. Your Doctrine is admirable, what doth other Folks faults concern us, let every body live as they please. But let us go on, and finish what we have begun, for methinks there is nothing so pleasing as love, and the Minutes we spend therein are the sweetest and most pleasant of our life. Hay for a good lusty standing Tarse, and a fine little plump hair Cunt, which affords us all these delights. I have but one question more to ask you, who are the most proper for love Concerns, Married Women or Maids?

FRANK. Married Women without question, for they are deeper learned, and have had longer experience in it, knowing all the intrigues of that passion perfectly well.

KATY. Why then do some Men love Maids better?

FRANK. Because they take pleasure to instruct the ignorant, who are more obedient and tractable unto them, letting them do what they please, besides, their Cunts are not so wide but fit their Pricks better, and consequently tickleth them abundantly more.

KATY. What is the reason then that others differ in this opinion, and choose rather to

Fuck with Women?

FRANK. Because as I have told you already, they have more art in pleasing, and the hazard is not half so great as with young Wenches.

KATY. What hazard to you mean?

FRANK. Of being got with Child, which is a Devilish plague to keep it private when the child is born, and besides the Mans Pocket pays soundly for it's maintenance, and the Woman shall have it perpetually hit in her Teeth by her Parents and kinsfolk, who will endeavor many times also to revenge it of the Man, if they have an opportunity; now if a Man deal with a Married Woman, there is none of this clutter, the Husband is the Cloak for all, and the Gallants children sit at his fire side without any expenses to him that got them, so that this security make them Fuck without fear, and enjoy one another the more freely.

KATY. So that now I have nothing more to do, but to get me a Husband that I may Swive without fear or wit.

FRANK. No marry ha'nt you, and when

you are so provided, as often as your Husband is absent or opportunities presenteth, you may Fuck your Belly full with your Friend, and yet you will love your Husband never the worse, 'tis only cheating him of a little pastime, and it is good to have two strings to ones Bow, and there is no doubt but you will be able to do them both reason, for there are few Men that are able to do a Woman's business, & besides change of Fucking as well as do it is very grateful, for always the same thing clothed.

KATY. Well then Cousin, since I have taken your instructions, and that by your means I have learned all that belongs to the mysteries of love, what will you say if I have some prospect of a Sweet-heart, whom I intend to make a Husband of?

FRANK. Do you ask my opinion if you shall marry?

KATY. Yes indeed, what else?

FRANK. Leave all that to my care, I am old & excellent at such a business, and 'tis Ten to one if the party care for thee never so little, but that I compass thy design and bring it about, I have here now gone through greater difficulties of that nature. Hark, the clock strikes, God be with you, we will speak of this more at large when we meet next.

KATY. God be with you then dear Cousin till I see you again.

FRANK. And with you too. Adieu, Adieu.

The end of the second Dialogue.

Quo me fata trahunt Nescio.

FINIS

Made in the USA
Las Vegas, NV
15 November 2023

80894214R00085